TARNISHED HEROES

Geoff Cumbley

Pen Press Publishers Ltd

Copyright © Geoff Cumbley 2006

Published in Great Britain by
Pen Press Publishers Ltd
39, Chesham Road
Brighton
BN2 1NB

ISBN 1-905621-01-9

Cover design Jacqueline Abromeit

About the Author

 Geoff Cumbley was born in Worcester at the beginning of the Second World War. His mother Lily was responsible for his early upbringing. The family was reunited when his father Jim returned from the conflict in 1945.

On completion of his education in the city he was employed in industry for several years. In 1967 he joined the Royal Air Force and achieved a twenty-two year engagement. On leaving the service he undertook a career in security.

He has travelled to the United States, Canada, the Mediterranean, the Middle and Far East.

Now retired he resides in Worcester with his wife Patricia. They have two children and two grandchildren.

TARNISHED
HEROES

To Dick,

With Best Wishes,

PROLOGUE

The winters seemed endless. Cold days and long dark nights, rain and snow no strangers to the English landscape.

Eventually spring arrived, new life came in the shape of lambs and calves. Gardens took on a refreshing change as flower beds were weeded, lawns mown and the vegetable patch accorded due attention. Thick ice on rivers and canals lost its grip, all kinds of boats sailed again. Anglers appeared to enjoy warmer days in pleasurable solitude. Churches became busy as the annual crop of weddings took place. Customers began to sit outside their local public houses, children drank bottles of 'pop' and ate Smiths Crisps.

Hot days and balmy nights prevailed as the summer season took hold. This was holiday time. Businesses closed for two weeks. Coaches, trains and cars headed for the coast. Hotels, guest houses and caravans filled with people searching for the perfect break from their working environment. Deckchairs became the day's haven on the beach. The younger element went for the eternal donkey ride, hard earned cash was spent at the fair and the evening found families gathered at their 'adopted' pub. Copious amounts of egg, bacon, cockles, muscles, ice cream, fish, chips and alcohol were consumed. All too soon the interlude was over and the population returned to their place of employment, the gates of industry flung wide to admit them.

Weekends saw leisure continue. Well-tended parks attracted many people of all ages. The youngsters played on the grassed areas with gay abandon. Music came from a bandstand to entertain people sat around listening or dozing

1

in the warm sun. The energetic tried their skill on tennis courts and others played the more genteel game of bowls on beautiful, fine-cut greens. Across the towns and cities the 'Sport of Kings' would be taking place. The horses would thunder down the race track increasing or decreasing someone's bank balance. Professional and amateur football was played throughout the land. The annual Wembley Cup Final provided great interest for the working man, especially when royalty attended for the first time. Many spectators took their seats at cricket grounds where they watched teams battle against each other for the County championship. Elsewhere, on village greens, the local teams continued an everlasting, almost feudal rivalry. Sunlit, peaceful hamlets came alive as willow connected with ball to be greeted by enthusiastic applause. In the pavilion a group of devoted ladies would be preparing cucumber sandwiches, lemonade and tea for the antagonists. The end of the game would see everyone troop off to the nearby pub where the cricket would be discussed over pints of ale and relationships would continue as before... until next year! Rugby Union and Rugby League Football attracted many sportsmen to its ranks. Hard men and others fleet of foot graced pitches all over the kingdom.

Church formed an integral part of community life. Regular attendance was encouraged in both city and countryside. Men of the cloth were prominent members of society, acknowledged as leaders and mentors. Come the Sabbath, church-goers wore their 'Sunday Best' to the services of their choice. Children attended Sunday School staffed by volunteer teachers. Parishioners maintained the church cleanliness and provided flowers. Church wardens carried out their respective duties – most of these would be part of the Parochial Church Council, a body of men and women who discussed all aspects of the establishment from functions to finance.

Christmas witnessed the nation's great family get-together. Weeks before the event decorations were made. Adults and children produced coloured paper chains which hung from ceilings or were draped over pictures. A real Christmas tree, holly and mistletoe were acquired along with paper hats and crackers. On Christmas Eve an air of anticipation reigned. The country's workers would be looking forward to the end of their toil; those who were on production lines would be waiting for their boss to appear to give the customary nod to signify an early finish, the pubs would be busy tonight. Christmas Day saw mums preparing dinner, and young and old alike would sit at the table and devour poultry, vegetables and varieties of inventive titbits covered in thick, brown gravy. This was followed by the 'good old Christmas pud', a concoction of fruit and spicy ingredients laced with spirits. Brandy was poured over the almost black substance and set alight, bringing forth cheers from the assembled group. Served in dishes with custard, the pud was eaten with care; some lucky person might find themselves grinding their teeth on a threepenny or even a sixpenny piece!

The afternoon would normally be a period of quiet, some adults drifting into a satisfied slumber. Christmas cake would feature at teatime. A rich, fruit cake topped with marzipan and icing, its presentation would be enhanced by a festively-decorated paper cake-band around its outside. Mince pies made their annual appearance, these would sometimes be reduced in number as children raided the kitchen! Drinks and games came into their own to round off the day.

Boxing Day arrives, this is the day of the foxhunt. The participants gather at pubs up and down the country. The Master of Hounds and his fellow huntsmen resplendent in red jackets take centre stage. The hounds – sturdy animals with a mix of white, brown and black coats – mill around, tails wagging in anticipation of the chase. The horses are beautifully groomed for this occasion. The followers gather attired in jackets, jodhpurs, highly-polished riding boots, the whole topped by appropriate headgear. A general hubbub of conversation takes place, then, at a given signal from the pub licensee, a tray of sherry appears, the first tot is offered to the Master who raises it to the assembled company before enjoying his tipple. Waiters scurry to and fro until everyone is served. Onlookers from town and city have come to see the landed gentry at play – this is the world of the farmer, the country squire, the educated upper class. The air of expectancy heightens and, at last, the Master leads the hunt out on a pre-ordained route. His destination is passed by word of mouth and anyone with a bicycle pedals away hoping to be in the vicinity of a find. If the spectator is extremely fortunate, his or her venture into the countryside could be well rewarded. The whereabouts of the hunting fraternity can be found as the Master sounds his horn at regular intervals. Hopefully a fox will break cover, the small brown body hurtling across the open field and the hunters emerging into full view, the riders crouched forward in the saddle their faces concentrated and determined, the horses at full gallop, their bodies moving with perfect co-ordination, manes and tails flying in the wind. Hooves thunder into the ground, the horn sounds, the hunters' shouting caught up in the wild pursuit of the quarry. The hounds speed forward barking as they go, adding their voice to the cacophony of sound. Soon the fox will go to ground; he may be cornered, meeting a swift end at the jaws of the dogs or he may slip out of a bolt hole leaving his tormentors empty-handed.

The hunt will continue for some time yet. The people on foot return to their families who are most likely waiting at a designated inn. Mums once again provide food; today's dinnertime fare is likely to be cold meat, pickled onions and mashed potatoes. Tea will be made up of bits and pieces, leftovers from previous repasts. Once again the pubs are open for business but this evening everyone is mindful that work will be waiting for them on the morrow, the yearly cycle will begin all over again.

The English, and many other nations, had been at conflict in the not too distant past. They had fought in the 'war to end all wars' and now a way of life had emerged with an agreeable mixture of work and pleasure and most thought that this would continue, but this was not to be.

The government of the day had adopted a policy of appeasement and only a few voiced their concern as military incidents took place in Europe. The German Chancellor Adolf Hitler was flexing his muscles and when he invaded Poland war was declared, the English would need all their courage and resolve to preserve their very existence.

Part One

IN THE BEGINNING...

ENGLAND 1939

Joe Thompson stood in front of a full-length mirror. Five feet six inches tall, blue eyes set in an oval face he sported a small moustache. He flicked a hair from the shoulder of his dark-blue pinstriped suit, checked his tie and adjusted his trilby to its customary rakish angle. Satisfied with his appearance, he opened the front door of his parents' house and stepped into the street.

Born in the cathedral city of Worcester located on the River Severn, Joe lived in the area known as St Paul's. The environment in which he was raised consisted of all types of dwellings, narrow streets, alleys, corner shops, innumerable public houses and business premises of various sizes. He attended the local school but was no scholar and left without any qualifications. Enquiries at local businesses revealed no job vacancies including the foundry where his father Charlie worked. In the end his mother Grace solved the problem. She sewed leather gloves for a Worcester-based company and knew one of its employees, Vera Lewis. Her husband George owned three general stores in the city and a conversation over a cup of tea led to Joe becoming an errand boy. He soon became a familiar figure pedalling through the city on his bicycle, the metal carrier stacked with goods.

Saturday night found Joe using the bridge over the canal, his target the 'Locomotive' pub. The landlord was behind the bar as he entered.

"Evening, Joe."

"Hello, Arthur, is she in?"

"Waiting patiently as usual," observed Arthur.

Pint in hand, Joe moved into the next room where he quickly found his girlfriend, Margaret; they kissed.

"Another drink?"

"Yes please," she said.

Joe stood with his back to the bar and surveyed the surroundings. He knew all the people present, one in particular! Ray Hopper was the local 'Bobby'. Their eyes met and they exchanged courteous nods of the head. Not so long ago Joe had decided to help himself to some sweets while his mother chatted across a shop counter. The sweets were in a jar and he had managed to grab a handful when a deep voice said,

"We could be seeing the start of a life of crime 'ere!"

Joe dropped the sweets as if they were hot cakes and spun round. Police Constable Hopper put on his most serious face.

"Dire consequences await those who thieve, is that not so, Mrs Thompson?"

"Quite right, Constable."

A moment later Joe recoiled as his mother clipped his right ear.

"Out," she said sharply.

As Joe left the shop, Grace glanced at Ray who winked and grinned broadly.

* * * * *

Nicknamed 'Hopper the Copper', Ray lived in a small house close to the canal with his wife Sally and his two children Geoff and Molly. Large in stature, Hopper had a round face, ruddy complexion, brown eyes with dark hair permanently cut short. A jovial character, he enjoyed a laugh with anyone. He had achieved his main ambition in life when the police force accepted him into their ranks and he felt that he had full control over his designated 'patch'. Some time ago he had embarked on a night patrol. He had glanced along an alley he was passing and stopped abruptly, someone was climbing down a drainpipe! Ray waited a moment then pounced, holding the shadowy figure in a tight grip. He met no resistance but when he moved his capture into the lamplight a shock awaited him – the person was Bob Hazelwood, a next-door neighbour! A shop next to the alley had been broken into, Hazelwood's pockets were found to be full of cigarettes, it was Ray Hopper's first arrest!

* * * * *

Brought up in one of St Paul's richer households David Collins was a spoilt child from the moment of his birth. Son of Harold, Maureen and brother of Margaret, he was his father's favourite. He wanted for nothing throughout his childhood. Margaret, too had the best money could buy but as David grew older he deliberately manoeuvred her into difficult situations and sat back with glee as his parents vented their wrath on his sister. David's education began at a school near his home but he passed the necessary examination to enter the local Grammar School. This was a real feather in his cap and he took full advantage, showing off his school uniform and books to anyone coming into the house. He adopted an air of superiority with his new classmates, but this did his popularity little good and one or two black eyes slowed him down, but not for long – he took his spite out on poor Margaret!

Although she loved her brother deeply, Margaret blessed the day he left home for University whereupon her life entered a period of peace and tranquillity. Her father planned to pass his antique business on to David and had carefully nurtured his interest and was delighted by his response but Margaret wondered if there was an ulterior motive in her brother's acquiescence, there usually was but soon all plans for the future would have to be put to one side as the clouds of war began to gather.

* * * * *

Twenty-six miles from Worcester is the great sprawling city of Birmingham. Here resided the Simmonds brothers, Mike and Tony. Their father Jim worked in a warehouse, their mother Jean took in ironing and needlework to supplement the family income. They lived in a two-storied terraced house in a dismal environment of old dwellings, occasional shops, pubs and grimy factories belching black smoke into the heavens. Theirs was a tough neighbourhood; police patrolled in pairs, ever watchful for criminal activity. At an early age the brothers became part of a 'gang' culture, this would remain with them into their teens. Their education suffered through poor attendance at school, they preferred to hang around on street corners, meander through the city, or fish in the canal which was used as a rubbish tip. Their teachers tried to instil learning into the boys by use of the cane or loud rhetoric but it was all to no avail. The boys, both thin, dark-haired with brown eyes, did everything together. They rose to joint leadership of a gang. Mike 'acquired' a football and organised games in the street. Jim gave them a pack of playing cards and gambling was added to their repertoire. Tony was a good climber and Mike acted as lookout while his brother entered premises searching for saleable goods. They became streetwise and were never caught by the authorities. Eventually, on leaving school they found employment on a building site. Both enjoyed the work and sought apprenticeship in the trade. They were successful, and on completion the brothers discussed going into business together but a radio broadcast by the Prime Minister Neville Chamberlain brought an abrupt end to that notion... for the time being!

* * * * *

Paul came as a late addition to the family. Peter and Elizabeth Parker were surprised by the pregnancy; they had not envisaged a child coming onto the scene. Well established in the community they lived in a quiet suburb, a clean unspoilt neighbourhood.

Paul grew up in this environment and was well cared for throughout his childhood. It was expected that he would follow in his father's footsteps at the bank where he was the manager but Paul had other ideas. As he grew older his parents had tried to encourage his interest in history. Visits to churches and museums failed to motivate him and his thoughts took him in other directions. There was another world, a place totally foreign to his present lifestyle and he wanted to be part of it. His school friends went to youth clubs and he persuaded his mother to let him attend one at the local church hall. Here he met people of his own age and developed friendships and widened his outlook. Paul met girls, smoked his first cigarette and one night he came home drunk. Peter and Elizabeth were appalled, especially when he vomited on the living room carpet! Things became very serious when Paul stated that he wanted to work at an engineering factory on the outskirts of town.

"And what brought this on?" asked Peter.

"All my friends are going there."

"I see, so this is your future?"

"This is what I want to do."

"Well, Paul, I think you could do better at the bank."

"I just can't see me sat at a desk."

Peter sighed, "Well, think about it and if the factory is where you want to go I suggest you try an apprenticeship."

Eventually Paul accepted the compromise. Peter's employment gave him a great deal of influence in the area and Paul's place in the factory was secured. He settled into the routine and for a time was quite happy, but the feeling of restlessness beset him. His instructor noted a lowering of Paul's standard of work and passed his observations to the young man in conversation. Paul wrestled with the problem inwardly, finally accepting the situation he found himself in, consoling himself with the thought that time was on his side, opportunities for change would come later. Halfway through his apprenticeship World War Two began, the Army beckoned, he responded.

* * * * *

The Victorian manor house sat in the centre of a large estate in the county of Warwickshire. Belonging to the Hilton family, the property was divided between arable farming and spacious gardens. The current occupants were ex-colonel Lionel, his wife Veronica and son Desmond. Lionel was from a long line of soldiers and this was reflected in the house décor – portraits of men in uniform gazed down from the walls, a painting of Lionel hung in the hallway. Lionel hoped that Desmond would follow the military way of life but vowed that he would not force the issue. Veronica persuaded Lionel to hire a teacher for the first years of Desmond's education and he agreed.

Mr Richard Dawson was in this forty-third year – a tall, broad man whose very stature demanded respect. Round of face, he kept his fair hair long, his blue eyes holding a mischievous twinkle. So it was that a fine relationship grew between tutor and pupil. Desmond especially enjoyed the summertime when he and Richard sat in the gardens with their books. He proved to be good with figures and language, French and German became part of his curriculum. Desmond's happy adolescence passed, soon he and Richard Dawson would part company. Brave faces marked an emotional farewell, Desmond went to his room, his mother and father understanding his feelings. One week later he entered the Royal Military College, Sandhurst.

During the next few years Lionel and Veronica saw their son ease into manhood. On visits home they enjoyed his intelligent conversation. His bearing became military. Square shouldered and upright, his demeanour especially pleased Lionel; it was Veronica who noticed the changed timbre in the voice. The life at Sandhurst suited Desmond. He enjoyed the mixture of militarism and learning. His instructors noted signs of leadership in his character, favourable reactions to discipline and his popularity with his comrades. One of his companions was Phillip Reardon. He too thrived at the college and often played Desmond at squash or badminton, they would talk and drink socially together.

It came as no surprise when the young Hilton successfully graduated from Sandhurst. His proud parents attended the ceremony and joined in the boisterous but friendly celebration. On that day no one could possibly foresee that the young men in the room would soon be plunged into world conflict... but that was their destiny!

* * * * *

Sheltered from life's hardships, Margaret Collins often felt embarrassed when with other people. She was well fed, well dressed and her home had all the modern facilities available, whereas most of her friends were less fortunate. Educated at a local girls' school Margaret worked at her father's antique shop where she performed bookkeeping and correspondence duties. She soon found that he had a large clientele of professional people for customers, and business continued unabated despite the war. By definition the Collins' circle of friends was small, comprising mainly of business associates. This, in turn, tended to limit Margaret and her brother David's relationships. Her contact with members of the opposite sex consisted of a mild flirtation with Joe Thompson either on the doorstep or in the 'Locomotive'. She was somewhat taken aback when he asked her to go to the cinema with him.

"I'll have to ask my parents, Joe."

"OK," he shrugged.

Margaret asked her mother, who looked at her apprehensively.

"I will mention it to your father."

"What?" said Harold, "He's nothing more that an errand boy for George Lewis!"

"Well I think we ought to go along with it, I can't see it lasting that long, he's way out of her league."

"Alright, my dear, play it your way, you're probably right."

To Harold and Maureen's surprise, Margaret's friendship with Joe blossomed. His presence gave them great displeasure and, to them, a lowering of their status in the immediate community.

Margaret went a step nearer to cementing her liaison with Joe, she wanted him to come to tea! Harold and Maureen were caught totally unaware. Silence reigned for some seconds before Maureen spoke.

"When, Margaret?"

"I thought Sunday would be nice."

"Yes that will be fine, shall we say four thirty?"

"Thanks Mum!"

Margaret skipped out into the street; Harold grunted and stomped into the kitchen, Maureen shrugged her shoulders, then followed him.

Smartly dressed, Joe sat looking around the drawing room. He took in the decor, the polished furniture, ornaments, mirrors, cushioned chairs and wall-to-wall carpet – opulence beyond his wildest imagination. Margaret reached out and took his hand.

"You alright, Joe?"

"Yes, why?"

"You look a little… bewildered."

"I suppose I am, our house is nothing like this."

Margaret smiled and kissed Joe on the cheek. Neither of them had heard the door open.

"Tea's ready," Maureen said.

Joe felt awkward, out of place here. He was used to eating in the kitchen at home, nothing as splendid as this. He was not alone in feeling uncomfortable, conversation was stilted and tea seemed to take an age. Margaret volunteered her and Joe's services in the washing-up department.

"Come into the front room when you've finished," said Harold.

The young couple were mostly silent, Joe was very careful with the china tea set. They could hear Harold and Maureen talking; it stopped when they were all together again. It was Harold who saved what could have been a disaster. He produced a pack of playing cards and drinks from his cabinet. The atmosphere noticeably changed and the rest of Joe's visit went relatively smoothly. Margaret brought the proceedings to completion.

"Joe and I are going to walk our tea down."

"Right," said Maureen.

"Good," said Harold.

"Thank you for tea, Mrs Collins."

"A pleasure, Joe."

"Bye, see you soon," Harold said.

Maureen watched the couple from the window, they were holding hands and laughing.

"They seem very happy together."

"Yes, what happens now?"

"Surely he will be called up soon to fight for his country like all his friends?"

"Let's hope so, Maureen."

Joe Thompson noticed the empty spaces in the 'Locomotive' bar; men were going to war and one morning his conscription papers duly arrived.

Grace simply held her son to her bosom and wept. It was with great reluctance that he made his way to the local recruiting office. He was processed accordingly, finally finding himself standing in a line of men who were likewise stripped to the waist. A doctor began his examinations. The stethoscope was cold and Joe jumped, the official looked at the ceiling.

"Mouth open... say arrh."

"Arrh!"

The medic turned to the sergeant accompanying him. He tapped Joe's chest.

"Not this one, asthma or something like it."

He turned to Joe.

"See a doctor!"

Joe's feelings toward his rejection were mixed but he soon discovered that other people had their own thoughts on the matter. Working for George Lewis had given him an opportunity to form good working relationships with local shopkeepers and assistants. Joe sensed a hostile atmosphere directed towards him, older employees avoided him, moving away as he approached. On the street people looked at him strangely and on one occasion a man spat on the pavement in front of him. This upset Joe, he told George what was happening. George considered Joe's predicament, stroking his well-groomed moustache.

"I think a little subterfuge is called for here."

"Oh?"

George explained and from that day on Joe carried a large handkerchief and developed a 'cough' whenever embarrassing situations presented themselves. Slowly word of his poor health spread sufficiently enough for near normality to return.

Margaret was passing the city recruiting office when she saw a poster in the window. It pictured a young woman smiling and waving with the words 'Help us to Victory – Apply Within'. Margaret hesitated, then purposefully strode into the building. She declared her interest to a woman behind a desk and, after a brief conversation, left, clutching a leaflet.

Maureen was in the kitchen baking when Margaret entered.

"Hello, dear."

She spotted the leaflet.

"What have you got there?"

"Information about women joining the war effort."

"And where do you fit into the scheme of things?" asked Maureen.

"The authorities are looking for female staff at Norton Barracks to work as cleaners, drivers or kitchen hands. With all able-bodied men disappearing, somebody has to fill the vacancies."

Norton Barracks was an army-training establishment on the outskirts of the city, home to the Worcestershire Regiment; Maureen struggled to visualise her daughter working in such an environment.

"What about your job at the shop?"

"Father could soon find someone else."

"I suppose you have an idea who that someone else might be?"

"Yes, mother, you!"

Maureen spluttered.

"Me?"

"Why not, you would soon pick it up."

Maureen hesitated.

"Leave this with me, young lady, I just don't know what your father's going to say!"

Harold pondered over the latest intrusion into his well-ordered routine.

"What a brilliant idea," he said.

Maureen could hardly believe her ears.

"Are you serious, Harold?"

"Yes, it would do us all good, a little show of patriotism would do us no harm at all."

It was these last few words that swayed Maureen. She allowed the idea to fester and actively began to encourage Margaret.

Margaret became a kitchen hand at the barracks where she met all types of people. Some of her companions were coarse, constantly swearing and recounting tales of drunkenness and sexual exploits, but she was impressed by their banding together in the face of adversity. Close relatives died in the battle for world peace and Margaret saw real pain for the first time. Loyalty stood out, the girls travelling through rain, snow and ice so as not to let their workmates down. She watched the recruits marching to and fro, orders bellowing across the parade ground. She got used to the rhythmic firing on the rifle range and winced at the blood-curdling yells of the men at bayonet practice.

One day, just after closing time, George called Joe into the shop and beckoned him to a seat. He took some money from the till.

"I want you to get two new padlocks, Joe – one for the street gate and one for the outhouse round the back."

"OK."

"I'm buying a van, it arrives on Monday."

He handed Joe a folded piece of paper, which he opened. It was a map of the county bearing eight crosses in red ink next to farm names. Joe looked up, puzzled.

"When you've finished your normal rounds I may ask you to go to one of these farms, there will be a load for you to pick up. I'm having the outhouse turned into a cold store and everything you collect can go in there. We must do this quietly so as not to draw too much attention."

"What's going on, George?" asked Joe.

"The government are issuing ration books soon. Some items of food and so on will be in short supply and I intend to fill these gaps. Certain customers will pay well for this service and you, Joe, will be paid accordingly. We'll have to keep the gate locked and an eye open for 'Hopper the Copper', what do you think?"

"Who knows, I could marry Margaret sooner than expected."

George smiled, the die was cast!

* * * * *

The Lewis business empire was founded by Percy. He undertook various projects, developing a knack of knowing when to move on. His union with his wife, Victoria, produced one son. He made sure that George was well educated and when he judged the time to be right he handed over the reins of power. George was more than surprised. Seated at the highly-polished table in the drawing room he received the deeds of his father's remaining grocery store, a set of keys and the knowledge that a princely sum of twenty-five thousand pounds was at his disposal.

"A piece of advice, George..."

"Yes, Father?"

"Build a list of contacts, give good service to your customers whoever they may be and keep your business legal."

George took heed of the advice; he became a member of the Worcestershire County Cricket and Rotary Clubs. Wisely he cultivated friendships with influential people and, as his father had said, opportunities came his way. Vera Partridge, the daughter of a business associate, came on the scene at a party. She was slim and graceful and socially well connected. Vera saw a future with George and allowed their friendship to rise to a level of courtship. They were married twelve months after their initial meeting. Although they were happy George soon discovered that Vera was a spendthrift. He kept tight control of their finances. Let Vera loose at the bank I'd be bankrupt in a week, he thought!

No children arrived at the Lewis household; medical examination revealed that Vera was barren. She and George talked at length about adoption but no decision was ever reached. George put most of his energy into expanding his business and lengthening his list of contacts. Vera took a job in one of the offices at Fownes glove factory close to her home. She gained financial independence this way but some of her extravagant purchases managed to raise her husband's eyebrows. Because of his shrewd business skills George could afford the luxury of two holidays a year, usually a trip to Europe. Vera loved these visits and there were always invitations of various kinds from the business fraternity or customers.

World War One disrupted life for most people. George served his country in France. He was wounded in the shoulder and Vera suddenly felt insecure. He returned to the front once more, to face the strong possibility of death. The postman became a figure to be dreaded, people sighed with relief when he walked past their homes and kept going. George survived the war but it had changed him. He kept the horror and privation locked away and it took all Vera's strength to bring him back to his pre-war demeanour.

* * * * *

George sat in the shop alone, pondering. He could hardly believe that a world war had come into his life a second time. He was also well aware that he was breaking one of his father's cardinal rules of business. Black marketing was illegal but here was an opportunity presenting itself. Farmers formed part of his clientele and he knew that they were short-handed and had no time to deviate from their chosen task. Bacon, butter and sugar were coming under the rationing hammer but he knew that this was the thin end of the wedge. Collection, distribution of goods and careful choice of customer formed George's business plan. He compiled a list of likely suppliers and recipients and set to work. George appreciated the danger of his venture but also the possible rewards. Business lunches, drinks, a few dinners and visits to his clubs resulted in veiled conversations. He carried a notebook and fountain pen as a matter of course. The book gradually filled and was locked away when not in use, he made sure Vera knew nothing of the new scheme.

Agreements reached, George brought Joe Thompson into his confidence as a necessity. The van was large but Joe mastered it and he began to drive in the early hours of the morning or under cover of darkness if the cold store was to be used. Quite soon after the operation began George hired a new errand boy leaving Joe free to concentrate on distribution. Margaret asked awkward questions but Joe managed to explain his new role without raising suspicion. He controlled his urge to spend extra cash and impressed George to the point where he showed Joe the one account book that contained details of their clandestine activities.

One problem gnawed at George's core – it came in the shape of Police Constable Ray Hopper. He was a profound danger to the set-up and would have to be dealt with. George decided boldness would be the best option; he didn't have long to wait to put his thoughts into action.

"Nice van, George."

Lewis hadn't seen him enter; he had his back to the shop while he was stacking shelves. He turned slowly, keeping his face expressionless.

"Hello, Ray, how's things?"

"OK, thanks."

He gestured behind him at the vehicle.

"I thought business would go down in war, George?"

"Still plenty of customers out there," said George.

"I don't see so much of Joe these days come to think of it, on nights is he?"

Alarm bells rang in George's head.

"Shops want their goods early these days."

"Yes, for all the customers they're going to get!"

George caught the sarcasm in the remark... he took a deep breath.

"Ray, how would Sally and the kids like extra bacon and butter this week?"

"We're talking about rationed items, George."

"Yes."

"I see, is this a bribe?"

"Could be it's a friendly gesture, Ray."

"I'll see you later, George," Hopper said, and walked out of the shop.

* * * * *

"George Lewis tried to bribe me today."

Sally looked up.

"What did he say?"

"He offered me extra bacon and butter."

"What did you say?" asked Sally.

"I didn't answer him... What would you have said?"

"I'd be tempted, Ray, things will probably get a lot worse."

"It's illegal, Sally!"

"Were there any witnesses to your little chat?"

"No."

"Then you have no evidence."

"That's not the point, Sally, if we touch this stuff we're as guilty as he is."

"Rationing will stop sometime, Ray."

He sat deep in thought, torn between loyalty to the police and his responsibilities to his family.

The following morning George Lewis was alone in the shop when Ray Hopper came in. Their eyes met, they were both on edge.

"Sally would like the 'extra's', George."

"OK, Ray."

"This conversation never took place."

"That's understood."

Hopper left the building, Lewis breathed a sigh of relief, no more obstacles, he thought.

Part Two

AFRICA: THE DESERT

AFRICA 1940

Captain Hilton, Lieutenant Collins, Corporal Parker and Privates Mike and Tony Simmonds became members of the same infantry unit, part of the British Eighth Army fighting in North Africa. Collins was Hilton's right-hand man, they conversed on many subjects with antiques usually the main topic. Hilton adopted a policy of consultation with the men under his command. He was able to create a fine balance between discipline and comradeship. Success in this method of leadership would reap their reward in the hard years ahead.

The allied forces began to attain victories over their Italian adversaries. One evening during a lull in fighting Hilton noticed that the Simmonds brothers were not with their usual group of friends. His questions as to their whereabouts were received with negative answers, he gave up. One hour later the brothers stumbled into the camp, their arms were laden with bottles and packages. Cheers rang out, Hilton and Collins hurried to find the cause of the commotion. The fruits of the Simmonds' mysterious disappearance were there for all to see – there was red and white wine and a sizeable quantity of pasta. Hilton positioned himself at the edge of the jubilant crowd.

"Privates Mike and Tony Simmonds – a word!" he said sharply.

There was a momentary silence as all eyes turned towards him, then conversation resumed unabated. The brothers followed Hilton and Collins until they were out of earshot of everyone else.

Hilton spoke, "I presume you have raided the enemy lines?"

"Yes, sir."

"Do you realise the ramifications of your action? Dereliction of duty, disobeying orders, desertion and theft to name but a few of the charges I could dig up against you, do you understand?"

The brothers looked at each other.

Hilton continued, "Well done, boys, a bottle of wine for the Lieutenant and I – before I change my mind... now get lost!"

The brothers departed, Hilton and Collins smiled.

The unit cook wove his magic on the pasta and dishes not usually connected with a soldier's diet appeared, the wine lasted but a short time.

To the allied warriors on the field of battle the 12th February 1941 was just another day but it was to prove highly significant in the months ahead. Lieutenant-General Irwin Rommel arrived to address the situation in the North Africa campaign. Not long after this event dramatic changes took place in the desert. Opposition to the Allied forces stiffened substantially. Faced with superior generalship, tactics and equipment, they were forced to fall back under the onslaught. Morale became seriously undermined. In very temporary accommodation Hilton vented his frustration.

"How do we stop this shambles, David?"

Collins shrugged, "Search me, it's all gone to pot since Rommel took over."

"Yes the 'Desert Fox' has made quite a difference," said Hilton, using the name respectfully reserved for Rommel by both sides. Just then came the unmistakable scream of incoming shells; the ground shuddered and dust fell from the ceiling as they exploded. Hilton grabbed his helmet and rifle.

"Here we go again, no rest for the wicked!"

Soldiers sprinted for prepared dugouts; some didn't make it. Hilton swore. The bombardment would only last a few minutes, enough to cause general disruption. It was dusk now but no respite was forthcoming, these attacks would continue at irregular intervals throughout the night.

Days passed, one blending into another as the war of attrition went on. On one occasion Hilton and his men were caught in open desert by a squadron of enemy tanks. Men scattered in all directions, fearing imminent death. Suddenly three aircraft roared into view, this was the end!

"They're ours," someone called.

Everyone stopped and turned. Machines of destruction descended from the sky. Mere mortals watched in awe as the aircraft systematically decimated the tank force, few escaping the assault.

Hilton said, "Thank god!"

"Unbelievable," said Collins.

Their momentary relief was soon replaced with consternation. Simmonds and Parker were among the wounded, Tony had been hit in the shoulder, Paul in the thigh. They were quickly patched up by medical staff before being transported to a field hospital. The seemingly endless retreat continued. Rommel's forces laid siege to the Libyan port of Tobruk; it eventually fell in June 1942. Hilton and Collins remained unscathed but lost men, mostly stragglers taken prisoner by the pursuing enemy.

The Allies found themselves near a place in Egypt called Al Alamein. Here the 'Desert Rats' turned, at bay, to face the might of the German and Italian foe. The battle raged back and forth over the sand. Probe and counter-probe, attack and determined defence. Men and machines that would never function again littered the battlefield. There were many close calls but the Allied line held and, at last, the Axis army withdrew to lick its wounds.

Hilton surveyed his troops. They were sat or sprawled on the ground but he noted that their rifles and ammunition were within easy reach. He strolled among them exchanging a few words, sometimes squatting for some moments talking to those he knew well. There was no celebration or feeling of elation. The Allied army slept well that night. No shells descended from on high to disturb the tranquillity.

Although the desert conflict continued, Captain Hilton and Lieutenant Collins sensed a profound change in their daily routine, they had stopped running! The enemy threat was still there but it seemed to lack impetus. One day a truck turned up with bags of mail. Starved with news from home, cheering troops waved bundles of letters in the air. Silence descended, Hilton couldn't remember such peace and quiet in daytime hours. It could hardly be expected that all the news would be good and their comrades consoled those who had received bad tidings. Hilton couldn't believe his luck. Two days later Tony Simmonds and Paul Parker, both fully recovered, rejoined the unit.

What next, thought Hilton? He did not have long to wait. August 1942 saw General Sir Bernard Montgomery become commander of the Eighth Army. 'Monty' was no dashing, charismatic Rommel, here was a tactical planner, a man who amassed superior forces before engaging the enemy. He had an inbuilt ability to communicate with his fellow man of any rank. It became common to see him conversing with a group of troops, his regulation uniform topped with the eternal beret, his hands clasped behind his back. He instilled confidence throughout the entire army, and obtained the men, ammunition and military machines he required to face Rommel on more than equal terms.

Explosions, flying sand, burning machines, men crying, men dying. This was the second battle of Al Alamein. The well dug-in Axis troops suffered an artillery barrage that seemed to go on forever. When it eventually lifted, the infantry came supported by superior air cover. Forced to keep their heads down, enemy soldiers were among them before they realised it. Shooting gave way to the bayonet. Systematically minefields were blown away, it was time for the tanks to make their move. Defences began to crumble under the assault, terrified men ran before these steel carriers of death. Rommel ordered his depleted, overstretched forces to retreat. Relentlessly his beloved Africa Korps were driven back to eventual obliteration in the spring of 1943. Hilton would always remember a quip by one of his men as summing up his own Africa experience. They were in completely open country when a corporal stopped and pointed.

"Look at that, I've passed that bush three times this year!"

Hilton smiled and trudged on.

Part Three

EUROPE: THE CONFLICT

ITALY 1943

In July 1943 Canadian, American and British forces invaded Sicily. Some five weeks later their Axis opponents had ended resistance. Early in September British troops crossed the Strait of Messina and landed on the toe of Italy. Captain Des Hilton, David Collins, the Simmonds brothers and Paul Parker were among this group. They were to experience all the seasons as the Italian campaign became a long, hard struggle. There was little time to admire the beautiful countryside, the German forces took full advantage of the terrain. Thick green vegetation hid machine gunners, tanks and infantry; ambush could come at any moment. Vineyards tempted the inexperienced soldier, mines claimed the unwary, booby traps created havoc. Narrow roads served to delay any swift advance, a tank or two with infantry and small arms provided a major obstacle, ravines provided the same problem and in mountainous regions the roads were hemmed in by steep cliffs. Still very active, the Luftwaffe constantly threatened from the sky. The enemy blew up every bridge they crossed. Engineers employed countless Bailey bridges. These were built under cover of darkness, some were damaged before completion and they had to be crossed under fire. Inevitably rain came, fields turned to quagmire, vehicles strayed off the roads at their peril. Roads collapsed under the weight of military vehicles.

Des Hilton worked hard to minimise the loss of men but his force continually took casualties. He exchanged views with Collins.

"I think I would rather fight in the desert."

"Me too, at least we had room and visibility."

"We could be here a while, David."

"No doubt, some will be here for good."

"Yes," said Hilton, soberly.

The next day a Colonel approached Hilton. Quick pleasantries were exchanged then the officer came to the point of his visit.

"I require six of your best marksmen, Captain, we need snipers, and quickly."

"How quickly?"

"One hour!"

"Right, sir."

Lieutenant Von Frober lead a patrol of ten men. They were in single file moving cautiously through trees and thick undergrowth. An expected enemy assault had failed to materialise and their location was vital to German intelligence. Von Frober was uneasy, it was too quiet. He looked behind him, his men were well spread out, looking left and right as they moved forward. He raised an arm and the patrol stopped and crouched down. He stood a moment, listening, not hearing the shot that ended his existence.

The patrol flattened themselves into the grass. Sergeant Peter Mueller lay still, waiting. He was unsure from which direction the shot had come, he waited some minutes before raising his head to look around. All was quiet, Mueller stood up, the men watched him for some seconds before they too got to their feet. Mueller made his way to where Von Frober had fallen. He lay spreadeagled on his back, his eyes open, unseeing. A neat hole in the forehead marked the point of entry, blood staining the grass beneath the head; practised fingers closed Von Frober's eyes and went through his pockets. Finding a map and pencil Mueller marked the patrol's position, motioned some men to pick up their officer and began the trek back to base.

The patrol had long disappeared from view, the only sound came as dew dripped spasmodically from the trees, then part of the green scenery was displaced as the sniper moved from his position. Heavily camouflaged, Paul Parker stared through the trees where the Germans had departed, there was no movement. Satisfied he returned to his own lines. Once there, he reported the incident to intelligence officer Major Phillip Reardon who marked the position on a map spread across a table; he straightened.

"Thank you, Corporal, well done."

Parker saluted, "Sir!"

A cool customer, thought Reardon.

Very slowly the Allied forces moved northwards into Italy. German opposition remained steadfast and the Allied cause was not aided when troops were withdrawn for the coming invasion of Normandy. August 1944 found Hilton and his troops in the vanguard moving to occupy the city of Florence in Tuscany that straddles the River Arno. Shelling heralded the arrival of another relentless battle. The attackers ground their way through rubble, machine-guns chattered, grenades exploded and rifle-fire crackled endlessly. The unmistakeable clank and whine of tanks drove men into cover; bazookas caused mayhem in the narrow streets. The German army retreated, systematically destroying bridges as they crossed the river, leaving only one intact – the world famous Ponte Vecchio. The city was secured, Hilton and his men were rested, many casualties had been sustained and replacements were required.

Des Hilton and Dave Collins revelled in the surroundings. The greater majority of prominent buildings had survived the battle. Florence is overshadowed by its cathedral, Santa Maria del Fiore, its exterior composed of red, white and green marble. The structure is topped by a huge dome completing a scene of architectural perfection and charm only matched by the cathedral's interior. Works of art by Italian, French and Flemish painters fill the Uffizi Gallery, Hilton and Collins spent two days here. Quite close to the gallery is the Ponte Vecchio, the home of jewellers' and goldsmiths' shops. The two officers buried themselves in antiques but they both knew that their time here would not last much longer.

It was on one of these sightseeing trips that Collins spotted a church at the end of an alley that might prove interesting. He strode away, Hilton strolling behind. He hardly felt the tug of the wire on his leg but he did hear the metallic click on the concrete. There was no escape, the grenade exploded under a flat rock cleverly angled upward. Steel fragments tore through trouser and flesh, Collins screamed in agony. Without thinking, Hilton turned and ran to the main street. It was some minutes before he spotted two soldiers with the familiar red cross on their sleeves.

"Medics!"

The three men arrived to find David Collins unconscious, the lower half of his body a mass of blood and mangled limbs.

He was falling through darkness; hands caught him and pushed him back to his original position. Pain knifed through him, it passed and he was back in an alley. He felt the tug on his legs and the telltale click on the floor, the same nightmare over and over again. Eventually David Collins returned to consciousness. A face came into focus, it was dark with black hair and rich, brown eyes. Collins noted the white, even teeth.

"Welcome back, Mister Collins. I am Doctor Gino Rinaldi, how do you feel?"

"I've felt better!"

Rinaldi nodded and two nurses lifted David into a sitting position.

"We will get rid of the shock now, I want you to know the truth from the outset," Rinaldi said.

Bemused, David looked down at his bed... Almost from the waist down the sheets were flat! Horror filled him and anger quickly followed. Doctor Rinaldi and his nurses listened to a tirade condemning the war, mankind and anything else he could bring to mind. Gradually the storm died and David lapsed into silence, an injection of morphine put him into a sound sleep. The next day went very differently.

"Where am I, nurse?"

"Florence Hospital."

"Do you all speak English?" Collins asked.

"No, not quite all," she said.

"Do you have a name?"

"Maria," she replied.

"You are very pretty."

"Thank you, sir," she curtsied.

Doctor Rinaldi appeared, white coat billowing.

"And how is my English patient this morning?"

"Ashamed, Doctor!"

"Your outburst yesterday was quite understandable, we've seen it before and no doubt will see it again. Have you eaten?"

"No."

"Maria, feed and water him we have his future to discuss."

David looked at him sharply, "You think I have a future?"

"That depends on you, David."

The war continued without David Collins. The Germans formed what was called the Gothic Line, this was overrun but the Allies could not vanquish their foes in time, they were forced to cease hostilities and spend a frustrating winter in the mountains. 1945 arrived and by April of that year the German Third Reich was in its death throes. Nuremberg fell and the Soviet armies approached Berlin. In the middle of the month American and British forces attacked and brought the contest in Italy to an end. Hilton, Paul Parker, Mike and Tony Simmonds stood on the bank of the River Po, the war was over for them. Des felt an overwhelming tiredness, perhaps even a feeling of anticlimax. There would still be duties to perform, but he and his warriors were going home.

In Italy German forces surrendered at Caserta on May 2nd. General Alfred Jodl signed the papers which endorsed the unconditional surrender of all German forces at Rheims, France, on May 7th; victory in Europe was declared the following day.

Part Four

THE HOMECOMING

It was late September that the news of David's catastrophe had come to the Collins' household. First a telegram arrived then, within hours, a letter from a Doctor Rinaldi in Florence. He briefly outlined how David's injuries had come about and that it would be possible to fit false legs. He would be confined to a wheelchair for the rest of his life but he, Doctor Rinaldi, would produce two fittings, which would enhance David's image. He pointed out that David was healing well bodily but he found it difficult to gauge the mental effect. He conveyed his deep sorrow and said he would make every effort to get David home by Christmas. Harold put the letter down slowly. He looked into the tearstained faces of his wife and daughter.

"He doesn't mince words does he?"

"No," said Maureen, her voice cracking.

"I suppose that is the best way, at least we have some idea what to expect."

This brought another outburst of tears and Harold quickly moved to embrace the girls.

"David won't want to see this when he comes home, at least he's alive!"

The ship tied up in the harbour at Southampton. The Collins family waited apprehensively as the passengers disembarked.

"There he is!" said Margaret, pointing.

A medical orderly wheeled David down another gangplank away from the rest. The family pressed forward.

Harold hung back a little as the ladies greeted his son. David took their kisses and pleasantries with a smile knowing full well that soon an awkwardness would prevail and questions would come sporadically, he looked forward to the end of the feigned cheerfulness and settling down into some sort of normal routine. Maureen and Margaret moved aside, Harold stepped forward.

"Hello, son."

"Hello, Father."

The two shook hands.

"How do you feel, David?"

"I feel very well, Doctor Rinaldi and his nurses worked wonders. I have two contraptions for legs and I even have shoes!"

"I noticed, now let's get you home."

Harold undertook to push the wheelchair, David himself released the brake. Harold was thinking, I noticed your shoes David, I also noticed something else, the smile might be there but your eyes are full of hate!

* * * * *

Des Hilton looked down at his de-mob suit.

"Very classy," he remarked.

"Chic," Tony Simmonds grinned.

They were on English soil, going home. Hilton had the addresses of the 'Desert Rats' who had survived and some of those who had fought alongside him in Europe.

"Maybe we could have a reunion later?"

A shake of the hands, a clap on the shoulder.

"Goodbye!"

"See you around!"

Hilton walked toward the bus station. He felt lonely, and experienced a huge sense of anti-climax. It was all over, years of fighting in different climates, fear, elation, privation, over indulgence, sorrow and above all, the camaraderie with his fellow soldiers. His thoughts came to the surface.

"Another chapter opens, I suppose!" he said out loud.

A middle-aged lady was going past at that moment. She looked at him, shook her head and hurried on.

"I bet he never saw much of the war, poor chap," she said under her breath.

* * * * *

Carrying their suitcases Mike and Tony Simmonds stepped out of the railway station and stopped. They gazed at the buildings around them. Some were intact but many were charred ruins. The brothers looked at each other with but a single thought. They managed to find a taxi and shared a mutual anxiety as they were driven toward their home. Parts of Birmingham were obliterated, roofless churches, houses blown in half, furniture and wallpaper left for the bulldozer. Smashed vehicles, a double decker bus on its side burned out. Areas had been cleared leaving great gaps, there were a few signs of rebuilding going on.

"Plenty of work for us, Tony."

"That's a fact," Mike nodded.

There were still signs of the bombing on the house, burn marks from flying debris, a cracked window pane, tiles missing and broken guttering. Mike knocked at the front door. When it opened their mother faced them, their father behind.

"Hello, Mum."

"Michael, Tony – come in, come in!"

The four of them moved into the house embracing, hand-shaking and kisses exchanged in the emotional atmosphere created by the brothers' homecoming. Jean stood back and looked at her sons.

"You're both thin, have they been feeding you?"

"Yes, Mum," they chorused.

"They look fit, Jean, we should be thankful for that."

"True, I'll put the kettle on," Jean said.

"You'll be wanting to get rid of those suitcases, off you go, nothing's changed."

"Right, Dad."

Once upstairs Tony voiced his concern.

"They look very old, Mike."

"It's been a terrible strain no doubt, we'll have to do what we can."

Later, gathered in the kitchen, stories were swapped. The brothers tactfully avoided the horrors of war at the front but listened to a catalogue of tragedy including the names of people they would never see again. Alone in their room again the brothers vowed to make a better life for their parents. The next morning found them searching the city for building work... It was a very short search!

* * * * *

Paul Parker's homecoming was unspectacular. His parents showed great emotion on his arrival and he was pleased to see them. He had looked up and down the street as he approached the house. The war had not been here, everything was neat and tidy as it always had been. Sat in his room, which was exactly as he had left it he thought about his future. The Army had made him feel useful, needed, but now the war was finished. Still thoughtful, he went downstairs.

"How about going out for a drink?"

His father looked at him.

"Your mother and I do not go out very often."

"I thought you might like to celebrate my return."

His mother reached for a decanter on the sideboard.

"We can do that here, dear."

Paul sighed, I'm going back into the Army, he thought.

He was reading a newspaper when the telephone rang.

"Hello."

"Is that Mister Paul Parker?" a male voice said.

"It is."

"Are you looking for a job?"

"Well… yes."

"How would you like to do the same work that you did in the army?"

Paul hesitated.

"You obviously know what I did."

"Of course but the pay is better and you get to travel."

"You seem to know an awful lot about me."

"It's our business to know, Paul."

"And if I want the job?"

"I'll give you a number to ring."

"Go ahead," Paul said.

He wrote the number down and heard the telltale click on the telephone, the caller had hung up. Twenty-four hours later he dialled the number.

"So you're interested?"

It was the same voice, for an instant Paul thought he recognised it.

"Yes."

"Good, you'll be needing tools, keep an eye out for the postman," the line went dead.

"There's a letter for you, Paul."

"Thanks."

He took the envelope to his room. He opened it to find a small flat key stamped with a number. A typewritten note told him that it belonged to a locker at the local railway station.

"Was the letter interesting, dear?" his mother asked.

"Just a note from one of my army mates."

"Is he alright?"

"Yes, he's offered me a job."

"That's good, dear, and so soon after you get back."

"I'm going out for a walk."

"OK, see you later."

Paul opened the locker and took out a brown suitcase with two keys taped to the handle. He managed to sneak the case to his room without being seen. He was immediately impressed with the contents. Set in shaped foam material were the parts of a rifle. He inspected each piece carefully before sliding the case under his bed. Paul waited patiently for his parents to leave him in the house on his own. Eventually they went shopping and he grasped the opportunity. He found the rifle easy to assemble; he felt the weight and balance.

"Perfect," he said aloud.

He picked up the telephone and dialled.

"Hello."

"Hello, Paul, is everything to your liking?"

"Yes."

"Instructions will follow in the post."

A package duly arrived. It was a cardboard box containing an amount of money in notes and explicit instructions. Paul studied these and then, at dinner, announced his imminent departure.

"But you've only just got home!"

"Yes I know, Father, but the job is overseas in the leisure business and well paid."

Paul had put his suitcases by the front gate. His mother kissed him.

"Come back when you can."

"Good luck, son."

A quick handshake and Paul was striding down the street. He did not look back, everything was as before, neat and tidy!

* * * * *

Des Hilton paid the taxi driver and walked up the drive to his home. He was quick to note signs of dereliction, overgrown bushes, unattended weeds, potholes in the road and a general atmosphere of decay. The house itself looked drab, roses had gone wild, the woodwork lacked paint and the windows were dirty. He knocked on the front door feeling acute trepidation. The feeling was justified. A man opened the door. He was tall, thin on top. His face was both wide and long, it was well worn, worldly. He wore a white shirt which had seen better days, a black, dusty waistcoat, corduroy trousers and a pair of unpolished boots. His blue eyes moved over Hilton.

"Yes, sir, can I help you?"

"Well yes, I live here."

The man fixed him with his eyes, stroking his chin.

"You mean you lived here, sir."

Hilton shook his head, perplexed.

"Would you be Mister Desmond Hilton?"

"I would."

"Ah, I'm caretaker at the moment, your house is going to be turned into a hotel, a development company bought it."

"So where are my parents?"

"At the Primrose Home for the Elderly, you'll be needing a taxi, 'ang on a minute."

The man disappeared leaving Hilton stunned by what he had seen and heard.

Mrs Walters, owner of the Home, looked across the desk at Des Hilton.

"You will find a great difference in your parents, life has not been kind to them."

"What happened?"

"To put it briefly all their employees went off to war, they couldn't cope with running the estate and it fell into ruin. Along comes a company who wants to buy it, Lionel had little choice."

"Is everything gone?"

"Yes, there is enough money available for them to stay here for some years but it may not be needed as you will see for yourself."

The military bearing was gone, Lionel was a shadow of his former self and his mother Veronica didn't know who he was. Conversation was difficult but Lionel confirmed what Mrs Walters had said. Des left the building and stood in the street pondering his next move. He felt totally alone in the hostile environment, his thoughts inevitably went back to his time in the army. Later he booked into a guesthouse, he needed time to think.

Part Five

THE ROAD AHEAD...

Joe Thompson proposed to Margaret, presenting her with an engagement ring composed of three heart-shaped diamonds.

"Joe, it's perfect!"

"Glad you like it."

She kissed him.

Maureen looked at the ring.

"Very nice, so it's official?"

"Yes, Mum."

Harold and David examined the ring and exchanged glances.

"It's a very nice piece of jewellery," Harold said.

The men retired to the drawing room leaving the ladies to chatter about the future.

"That's a very expensive ring, Dad."

"Yes, I know."

"It is genuine isn't it?"

"No doubt in my mind," said Harold, "He must be doing well with George."

"Yes," David frowned, "very well indeed."

* * * * *

David Collins returned to work in the antique shop. From its front window he gazed at the Grammar School. He realised how small his world had become. We'll have to change that, he thought.

Planning for the future appeared to be on many people's minds, particularly the Collins and Thompson families. Joe found a small house for himself and his prospective bride. Margaret's thoughts turned to a wedding dress and who she would choose as bridesmaids. Joe favoured the nearby Holy Trinity Church for the service and Harold suggested the Great Western Hotel, which was nearly opposite, as the venue for the reception.

"Hope it doesn't rain," Maureen said.

"Wisht, woman," said Harold.

Vera Lewis was not to be outdone in coming events. The country was set to celebrate the end of the war with street parties and she took on the advertising and organisation for St Paul's, chivvying both men and women into offering their services.

The month of May arrived. Vera Lewis was busy finalising her project and Margaret's excitement was growing. Maureen was fussing about trying to give an impression of being in full control. Margaret gave up her job at Norton Barracks, she would return to her father's shop, releasing Maureen to look after the family's domestic needs. It was not a sad parting, all her close friends were coming to the wedding!

Party day arrived blessed with warm sunshine. Vera Lewis looked at the sky.

"Thank you, Lord," she said.

She hurried down to the street but she need not have worried. Helpers moved to and fro. Tables, chairs and tablecloths appeared. Bunting was slung across the street; windows were bedecked with Union Jacks. Paper cups and plates arrived followed by a variety of food – all types of sandwiches, large and small cakes, jelly, blancmange and fruit were brought out. Containers of beer, lemonade, orange squash and cups of tea provided liquid refreshment. People began to fill the streets; excited children carried small flags and balloons. The vicar of St Paul's stood and made a welcoming speech and the party began. Vera Lewis looked about her, pleased by what she saw. Laughter filled the air, friends chattered as they consumed the fare. Someone had carried out two armchairs. They were occupied by an elderly married couple that lived close by. The man wore a grey striped suit complete with waistcoat, his shoes were unpolished and he sported a battered old trilby that barely covered his white hair. His companion wore a skirt and jumper covered by a flowered pinafore, her shoes were well worn and she had a headscarf, turban style, to top the ensemble. Both were eagerly supping beer from pint-pots!

George Lewis had supplied a gramophone and people linked arms, singing and swaying rhythmically to the sounds of George Formby, Gracie Fields, Vera Lynn and many others. They got up to dance, the children running freely among them enjoying the atmosphere. The party began to break up as pub opening time approached but those who left graciously thanked Vera for her efforts. People helped clear the street and it soon returned to its usual condition but the memory would remain for years to come, captured by numerous cameras present.

The next day, Sunday, saw the vicar struggle out of bed. He was five minutes late starting the eight o'clock communion service. He rubbed his bleary eyes and took in the scene. Very few of his flock were present and he wondered why he had made the effort to get here but he pushed the thought away, cleared his voice, and sallied forth into the day's proceedings. Tea, toast and two aspirin aided his recovery later. Everywhere was quiet, only the hard-core drinkers made the pub at lunchtime but the evening session showed a marked improvement.

With the wedding but a few days away, final arrangements continued apace. Maureen had a list of things to do and

45

regularly reviewed the situation. If Harold thought he was not going to be involved she soon destroyed that theory. There would be eighty guests and he would be called upon to help the best man with some chauffeur duties. He was designated to pick up flowers and buttonholes from the supplier and other little chores as they cropped up. Maureen liaised with Grace Thompson and found her very helpful and down to earth, this would be the beginning of a lasting friendship. Margaret and her bridesmaids had their final dress-fitting. Maureen checked her list. Everything was in place, from now on timing would be all-important. Friday came quickly and Joe and Margaret spent their stag and hen nights pub-crawling in the city, fortunately they managed to avoid each other. Margaret felt quite good as she went to bed but Joe was pleased that the wedding would be in the afternoon, his bedroom ceiling was spinning wildly and a bowl was strategically placed in case of accidents!

Maureen was content. Her daughter looked stunning, her dress was perfectly tailored, traditionally white with a lace veil, white shoes completing the picture. She had to admit that Joe looked very smart in his charcoal-grey suit. His hair was neatly cut, his shoes highly polished. Both he and Margaret took their vows audibly and when the service was over someone had procured some confetti and the bride and groom were suitably showered. The reception went well. Speeches came and went and everybody relaxed, the guests enjoyed the food, drinking and dancing. At some stage the bride and groom had changed their attire and the goodbyes began. They had a very short journey to the station but the car was still decorated with the usual wedding paraphernalia, tin cans bouncing on the road. Joe and Margaret boarded the train. He opened the carriage door and bowed.

"After you, Mrs Thompson."

"Thank you, Mister Thompson."

Joe turned and he and Harold shook hands warmly.

"Look after her, Joe."

"No problem, Mister Collins."

"Harold, please."

"Right... Harold."

The train pulled away and Harold and the happy couple exchanged waves until they were out of sight. It'll be one big anticlimax at home now, Harold thought as he left the platform, Maureen will be fretting for a week... He was so right!

* * * * *

David Collins sat behind the desk. He was office man in place of Margaret. Her administration system was good and easy to operate. His father was talking to a customer; David was checking some paperwork.

"Hello, David."

"Good grief, Des Hilton!"

They shook hands, Hilton looking at the wheelchair.

"How do you like my chariot, Des?"

"I'm sorry, David."

"No need to be, it wasn't your fault."

Harold came in, he nodded.

"This is my friend Captain Des Hilton, this is my father Harold."

The men shook hands.

"Take a seat, Des, tell me all."

Harold left them to talk; they were still talking when it was time to close the shop.

"Have you anywhere to stay, Des?"

"No, I'll have to find a guest house somewhere."

"That you won't," Harold said, we can put you up quite easily."

"Thanks, I've got a toothbrush!"

Harold was alone in the drawing room when David wheeled himself in.

"Have a drink with me."

"Right."

Harold watched David pour a whisky.

"Is everything alright, David?"

"As well as it can be at the moment."

"Do you have any idea for the future?"

"That depends on you, Dad."

"Oh, why me?"

"Have you ever considered retiring?"

"Never thought about it, am I in the way?"

"Frankly, yes," David said.

Harold was nonplussed by his son's words.

"You want absolute control, don't you like the way I do business?"

"The business needs a new hand on the tiller, there are new horizons out there."

Harold was angry, shocked by the turn of events.

"And what about your mobility, who's going to do your running about for you?"

"Des Hilton."

"Hilton, what does he know about antiques?"

"Quite a bit, he has a great knowledge of paintings and speaks German and French."

"A bigger asset than me, obviously."

"Put like that... yes he is."

Harold exploded, his outburst referred to the work he had put into the business, his customer relations and how it had provided for the family over the years. David sat stone-faced until his father ran out of steam. At that point Maureen came into the room. Harold was red in the face; David, outwardly calm, took a mouthful of whisky.

"What's going on?"

"Our son wants me to retire, he thinks that my business methods are outmoded and he wants to bring his friend Hilton into the shop!"

"Is that right, David?"

"Yes, Mother."

"I think we all need to cool down and think about things a little more clearly."

"Sounds right to me," David said, moving for the door. He went to his room leaving his mother and father to discuss the matter. The following day the atmosphere at the shop was tense. Few words were exchanged and everyone was pleased to see closing time. Dinner continued in the same vein but when everything was cleared away Maureen asked the menfolk to gather in the drawing room. She closed the door sensing the air of hostility, she remained standing.

"Your father and I have talked at length about what has been said and, hopefully, we can reach a compromise."

David moved in his seat, hand on chin, waiting.

"You would agree, David, that you know nothing about your father's customers."

"That is true, yes."

"We therefore think that Harold should take over a consultancy role for the time being."

"With regard only to customer relations?" David said.

"Yes."

Grim faced, David and Harold looked at each other. It was David that broke the ice. He smiled and extended his hand. There was a slight pause before Harold took his son's hand.

"Good luck!"

"Thank you, Father."

Maureen looked at each of them in turn. Things between them will never be quite the same, she thought.

Joe and Margaret came home. They appeared to be very happy and had enjoyed their honeymoon. Margaret listened to her mother as she outlined the new set-up at the shop.

"Who is this Des Hilton?"

"He was with David throughout the war."

"Where is he?"

"Visiting his parents at the moment but he has been staying here."

"And now?"

"He has found a flat close to the shop."

"What's he like?"

"He's OK you'll get on, no problem."

David invited Joe round for a drink. He was a little apprehensive; he had always felt inferior to David. His host was friendly enough; he poured Joe a brandy and engaged in some small talk enquiring about Margaret's health and so forth. Joe sensed that the reason for David's invitation would not be long in coming, he was not disappointed.

"What do you actually do for George Lewis?"

"I distribute goods to shops in the city just as I've always done."

"And?"

"And... nothing."

"I'm afraid I don't believe you, Joe, you work very strange hours for a normal business these days, what with rationing going on."

Joe did not reply. David carried on.

"Look, Joe, You're a member of the family now – if you are up to something we could all be in trouble, especially Margaret!"

David's final barb struck home, Joe visibly wilted.

"George and I are in the black market business."

David smiled, a smile of deep satisfaction.

"Tell me how the system works and, before you say anything, leave George Lewis to me."

Joe hesitated at first but knew that David would stop at nothing to get the truth; he began to talk.

"There's a call for you, Michael."

"Who is it, Ma?"

"Somebody called Desmond."

"Hello."

"Hello, Mike, it's Des Hilton."

"Good grief, hello, sir... Des, how are you?"

"I'm OK what are you doing these days?"

"Tony and I are back on the building work."

"I'm working with David Collins at his antique shop in Worcester, I thought you might pop down to see us."

"How is he?"

"He's in a wheelchair, the grenade took most of his legs away but he is as sharp as ever."

"Well that's something, give me your telephone number Des, we'll arrange a meeting very soon."

"OK, Mike, bye for now!"

One week later Mike borrowed a car and drove, with Tony, to the Faithful City.

"Hello, boys."

The men shook hands and Des sat them down.

"Drinks, lads?"

"Yes, sir," the brothers chorused.

Des relished the company as conversation took hold and they began to reminisce. Eventually they all felt peckish and went to a nearby fish and chip shop. When he'd finished eating, Mike glanced at the newspaper wrapping.

"I see we have a new Prime Minister."

"Yes, I wonder how Mister Churchill feels now?"

"He'll be back," Mike said.

The following morning found the threesome outside the Collins' home, Maureen opened the door.

"Good morning, gentlemen, do come in."

They all filed into the drawing room where Harold and David waited. Introductions over, all eyes turned to David. Mike and Tony stepped forward to greet him both averting their eyes from his legs. Once the initial meeting was over the atmosphere visibly relaxed, Harold's usual ploy of opening his drinks cabinet worked again, David in particular looking at his father with gratitude. Joe and Margaret arrived, and the house was to be a hive of activity for the next few hours. Maureen constantly flitted between the group and the kitchen, pleasant smells began to permeate the building and soon Margaret went to help her mother dish up the food. Dinner went very well, everyone voiced their approval of an excellent table. Maureen was pleasantly surprised when the brothers volunteered to wash up while Margaret put everything away. Later the ladies left the men to their talk and retired to the kitchen. Time went quite quickly, the ensemble enjoyed a light tea and trooped off to the 'Locomotive' to complete the day's proceedings. They had been sat a while when David turned to Mike.

"How are things going in Birmingham?"

"It's going to take time to rebuild, it's a hell of a mess in the centre. The war took as much out of our mother and father as it did us, but Tony and I get what we can for them."

"It must be difficult with rationing still with us?"

Mike leaned forward, looking around to see if anyone was in hearing distance. He lowered his voice.

"You remember Major Reardon who spent most of the war working in HQ?"

David nodded.

"Well, he finished up as a Colonel. He lives just outside Birmingham and runs a black market scheme from there."

"How do you know this, Mike?"

"Tony and I did a quick roofing job for him and we got a bonus – pairs of nylons and even a couple of cans of petrol. He really has some pull in the area."

"Sounds promising!"

Des interjected, "I know him, we were friends at Sandhurst, he was never short of cash."

David lapsed into deep thought, hardly tasting his beer.

"Can you and Tony come to the shop tomorrow?"

"Of course."

"Yes, shall we say about eleven?"

The four men sat around the office table.

"I would like a chat with Colonel Reardon, can you arrange it, Mike?"

"I don't see why not, what do you have in mind?"

"I think rationing will go on for some time and I reckon we should grab a slice of the cake while it's there. We could suggest Reardon widens his business if he has the contacts and resources."

"Right, David!"

One week later Des drove David to an address in Northfield, Birmingham. The house was large, perched on a knoll it dominated the surrounding area. Mike and Tony had already arrived. Phillip Reardon came out to meet his visitors as Des helped David into his wheelchair. Tall, athletic, dressed in army-type pullover with well-creased grey trousers and black shiny shoes the blue-eyed, short-haired Reardon looked every inch the military man. He smiled, revealing white even teeth.

"Hello, David. Hello, Des, come in."

The house mirrored its owner. It was well furnished with a mix of old and new styles. Both David and Des noted a few pieces of interesting antiques. One or two toys declared the presence of children, small pictures and a vase of flowers displayed a womanly touch. Phillip read their thoughts.

"Mary and the children are visiting their grandmother in Cheltenham at the moment so we won't be disturbed... drinks, gentlemen?"

Once everyone settled, David opened the conversation.

"Is this room quite secure, Phillip?"

"Yes."

"We are led to believe that you can obtain certain items that are in short supply at the moment."

"That is true, why?"

"Maybe you would be able to widen your field of business with a bigger distribution area, Worcester, for example."

Phillip said, "Go on."

"We can only supply certain items, you have a far wider choice than we do."

"I take it you have the organisation together already, David."

"Not yet, but soon."

"I see, and the method of transportation?"

"The Birmingham to Worcester Canal, it's right on our doorstep and less obvious to a passer-by."

"True, what about communication?"

"Coded telephone messages or letter."

"What do you suggest now?"

"We go home, think about the plan and arrange another meeting to pool our ideas, but no one is under any obligation. I'll give you a call in about three weeks, how's that?"

They all nodded and the meeting broke up.

George Lewis and Harold Collins had been friends for many years and he saw no problem in a meeting arranged by Harold's son David, he assumed it concerned antiques. Seated comfortably with a whisky, George watched David replenish his own glass.

"I will come straight to the point, George, I wish to purchase your shop and yard here in St Paul's."

George was startled, the whisky sloshed wildly in his glass until he regained some composure.

"Of course I would also need the books and your list of customers."

George studied David wondering how much he knew about the business.

"Have you been talking to Joe?"

"Naturally, he is my brother-in-law now, you know."

"Yes, David, and what if I say no?"

"A visit to Ray Hopper's superiors would blow your scheme into oblivion, George, and you with it. My way everybody wins – you retain two shops, your half of the coal merchants' and cash in hand from my proposition."

George looked into David's eyes. He shuddered at what he saw.

"You would shop us all wouldn't you, David?"

"With no hesitation, George; think about what I said, but don't take too long."

"How long, David?"

"Twenty-four hours should be enough. Finish your drink, I'll see you out."

"What sort of offer are you making financially?"

"There's no offer, George, what you get will be more than generous."

George stood in the street holding his trilby. He felt isolated; he looked at the Collins' firmly-closed door and walked slowly away towards his home.

* * * * *

On the left bank of the River Seine in Paris a party was in full swing. Windows were open, all lights were blazing and music belched forth. The atmosphere was smoky and people were chatting in groups or gyrating to the music. It was the early hours of the morning before the party broke up. One particularly good-looking young man emerged from the building. He paused to light a cigarette but he would never smoke it. His body suddenly pitched backward, sprawling across the pavement. More partygoers came and laughed and pointed drunkenly at the fallen figure then a woman's scream split the night air, she had seen blood on his face and his eyes staring blankly into space. Minutes later sirens announced the arrival of an ambulance rapidly followed by a police car. A quick examination revealed that the victim had been shot in the forehead. Partygoers identified him as Louis Debois, a printer, single and well known in the district. At first the police were puzzled as to a motive for the killing but a subsequent search of the Debois' apartment uncovered a rifle, ammunition and leaflets denouncing the French President, Charles de Gaulle. No one was ever charged with the murder.

* * * * *

Vera Lewis looked at her husband.

"Is there a problem, George?"

"No… why?"

"You're very quiet, not your usual self."

"I've sold the shop and yard to David Collins."

"What… when?"

"He came to see me on Friday, I agreed the sale yesterday."

"That was quick."

"Well, the offer was generous, I could hardly refuse and it does mean we can go to Europe again now the war is over."

Vera smiled, "You could retire altogether, George."

"The thought had occurred to me," he said.

David Collins invited Ray Hopper to take a seat.

"I will come straight to the point. I have bought George Lewis's shop and yard."

Ray visibly paled, Collins smiled.

"Of course I know about your little 'gifts' but I want to change things."

Ray sat up in the chair, wondering.

"I think a payment of cash, shall we say monthly, would be a far better arrangement don't you think?"

Ray found his voice, "I suppose so, David."

"No suppose so, Ray, our lives and careers could come to an end with one slip of the tongue, is that not so?"

"Yes."

"I think we understand each other, let's enjoy a drink and chat about something much more pleasant… how are Sally and the kids?"

Ray was sat in his chair deep in thought. Sally caught his mood, "What's up, Raymond?"

He turned to look at her, she could see pain in his eyes.

"You will find out soon enough, David Collins has bought the shop and the yard off George Lewis."

"Oh!"

"There won't be any more 'gifts'; he's going to give me a monthly cash payment."

"And what do you have to do?"

"Keep my mouth shut if I see anything out of the ordinary."

"So there's no real change."

"There is, I'm in deeper than I ever wanted to be."

Sally went to her husband and put her arms around him.

"Maybe there's a way out," she said.

"Let's hope I can find it."

Phillip Reardon considered the draft plans put forward by David Collins and Des Hilton. The Collins' antique empire catered for people with money. Two lists were produced, one of Reardon's products and one of David Collins' customers.

"You know all these people, David?"

"I know who I can trust."

"How many?"

"Three quarters of them."

"That's good, very profitable, I take it no one has been approached yet?"

"That's correct."

Who is going to work your end?"

"My brother-in-law Joe Thompson will retain his place as distribution manager, Mike and Tony will handle the barge, Des will look after the administration and communication side of the business. I have to look after the shop to allay any suspicions at home, Father will cover for me if he thinks I am going out on antique business, my sister Margaret runs the office."

"Any local police?"

"Taken care of."

"I hope you're sure of that, David!"

"Now you have to trust me, Phillip."

Reardon smiled, "OK, so canvas your customers and I will see what I can do."

When they were alone David turned to Des, "How does he get to know about all this available surplus?"

"You're an antique dealer with lots of customers, he's an accountant with lots of businesses."

"Ah, I begin to see."

"Statistics and analysis come second nature to him, hence his success in the army."

"Very neat."

Des nodded, "Yes, very neat!"

David Collins burnt the midnight oil, his task to list those people he would approach with the black market scheme. It was not easy, there had to be enough interest to justify the operation taking place and the question of cost would be most important. A new day had dawned when David was satisfied; he rubbed his eyes and went into the kitchen to make coffee. No doubt his mother and father would be up and about soon, he would have to look fresh for them – a quick wash and shave proved enough to give the impression that nothing out of the ordinary had occurred. Later, at the shop, he began to make appointments in the city and beyond. He made sure Margaret was busy before he spoke quietly to Des Hilton.

"I have a lot of visits to make, Des, you will have to cover for me; as far as I'm concerned it's all antique business, OK?"

"Right, when are you starting your rounds?"

"Now, I managed to get a car and driver."

"Good luck."

"Thanks, Des."

Margaret looked up.

"Where is David off to, Des?"

"He has several business appointments he said."

"Well that's charming, do you know who he is seeing?"

Des shook his head, "Not a clue!"

Margaret frowned, "Typical David, I suppose he may bring me up to date sometime."

He never did!

Maureen Collins was sat in her favourite chair reading when Margaret came in. She rose quickly, kissed and embraced her daughter.

"How are you ,dear?"

"Pregnant, Mother!"

Maureen stepped back in surprise, a hand covering her open mouth.

"Are you sure?"

"Doctor confirmed that I'm three months with child."

Maureen smiled. "What did Joe say?"

"Oh, he's over the moon, he's talking about taking his son fishing, football, all sorts of things."

"He's counting his chickens isn't he?" said Maureen.

"Oh very good, Mother." Both women laughed and embraced again.

"Where's Father?"

Maureen grabbed Margaret's hand, "He's in the garden, let's go and tell him the news!"

David displayed great pleasure when learning of his sister's pregnancy and made a great show when congratulating Joe, but he secretly thought, well, that will be Margaret out of the way, Des can take over her chair!

* * * * *

59

The barge came out of the night. Silently it slid under the canal bridge and pulled into the side. Joe and David watched the Simmonds brothers secure her. They shook hands.

"Where did you get her?" David asked.

Mike replied, "A basin in Birmingham, she's only two years old and runs on diesel, plenty of space and as sound as a bell."

"Good."

"Do we have a business to run?"

David smiled, "We most certainly do... did you bring some samples?"

"We did."

"OK, boys, Joe has the van, I'll leave you in his capable hands but remember, if there is a problem I need to know about, get to me through him, alright?"

The brothers nodded, David glanced briefly at Joe then disappeared into the surrounding darkness. That same day David received a letter from Gino Rinaldi. He had married the pretty nurse, Maria and still lived in Florence where he was building a practice. He hoped that David and his family were well and among other things he mentioned the war damage and a severe lack of drugs. For a few moments David experienced his personal disaster all over again but then returned his mind to the letter. He owed Rinaldi a great deal of gratitude. He and his nurses had brought about his recovery in body and mind, maybe he could do something to repay his debt. David reached for the telephone...

Later in the day a telephone call from Mike Simmonds confirmed that he and Tony had successfully completed the run from Worcester to Birmingham in daylight without any problem. Phillip Reardon would now work on a list of required items, the barge would soon be loaded and making its way south again.

* * * * *

They were in Reardon's drawing room.

"One big consignment to Florence, you say, David?"

"Yes."

"You certainly want me to stick my neck out!"

"I owe Rinaldi, I have to do something."

"I understand, David, how is this going to be paid for, expenses will be high?"

"I am prepared to foot some of the cash but Rinaldi will have to help."

"Right, David, contact him as soon as possible, I am off to Nuremberg next month so I need all the information I can get."

"Nuremberg?" queried David.

"Alleged German war criminals are to be brought to trial. All my interrogation reports will be on hand so that I can feed any information required to the lawyers and their associates."

"How long will you be away?"

"That's a good question, David, but do not worry, use the Simmonds boys to carry messages and arrange timings and so on, I will set up a contact at the Birmingham end."

* * * * *

Built on the Pegnitz River in Bavaria, Nuremberg was an old but battered city. During the war aeroplane, submarine and tank engines had been produced here and had provided a natural target for Allied bombing raids. Now its history would include the acts of retribution to be carried out against those who had perpetrated the horrors of war. Phillip Reardon was given a small office, which contained two chairs, a desk and filing cabinets. He immediately set about re-reading files and often faces from the past brought back memories, most of them not good. His accommodation was a small hotel not too far from the court building. That evening he enjoyed dinner and strolled into the bar.

"Hello, Phillip."

Phillip turned, smiling as he did so. The voice belonged to Frenchman, André Dupont. The men shook hands vigorously, they had met and worked together regularly in the field of intelligence. Reardon looked at André, nothing had changed, the full head of grey hair, the well-tended beard, the suit, collar and tie and the blue eyes that seemed to dance and sparkle with life, just as Phillip always pictured him.

The comrades sat at a table in the corner of the room, André preferred to hold conversations in the open.

"Rooms can be bugged!" he always said.

Pleasantries were exchanged and dispensed with.

"What's new, André?"

"Not a lot, the war may be over but there is still plenty of sorting out to do."

He lowered his voice, "Government send their thanks for the job in Paris, there will be others."

Phillip nodded.

"Are you still in the intelligence game, Phillip?"

"No, I have my fingers in a number of businesses in Birmingham."

"Legitimate of course."

Their eyes met, they both laughed.

"Our heads of state would like to show more appreciation for your work with us, is there anything we can do?"

"I need an aeroplane," Phillip said.

André Dupont's face remained impassive.

"From where to where?"

"Birmingham to Florence."

"Cargo?"

"Medical supplies."

"Why not officially, Phillip?"

"A private arrangement and a debt repaid."

"I see, give me a few hours."

"Thank you, André."

"Don't thank me yet, come, let's talk of pleasant things and enjoy a drink or two."

There was a November chill in the air but the two friends were totally relaxed in each other's company and Phillip went to his room later feeling elated by the day's events.

Gangling, loose tie, clothes ill-fitting, thinning hair, a long face with blue eyes and a moustache, this was ex-Group Captain Geoffrey Arnold, Royal Air Force.

"A pleasure to meet you, Mister Reardon."

The two men shook hands; Phillip glanced at André.

"I've spoken to Geoff about your requirement."

Arnold let his long frame drop into an easy chair.

"Come on, lads, let's have a drink."

The trio were in some sort of officers club formed for the duration of the trials. Arnold sat, fingers steepled, his voice was firm but low.

"When do you require this aircraft?"

"As soon as I can get home and organise a consignment."

"Right I have a Dakota C-47 – that do you?"

"Perfect!"

"Good, get your stuff together, sort out a landing area in Florence and off we go!"

He gave Phillip a business card.

"My contact number, speak only to me."

Arnold stood up, "I must away, gents, I have a date."

A quick shake of hands and he departed, his long striding walk soon taking him out of sight.

Phillip sat down, "Some character, what's he doing here?"

"He's an observer for the Royal Air Force looking at the Luftwaffe side of things, no doubt. Flew Spitfires in the war, quite a brain under that untidy appearance."

"Yes," agreed Phillip.

Part Six

THE ITALIAN FACTION

It was mid afternoon, the sun beat down on the large, old two-storied villa; its spacious gardens were filled with flowers, bushes and trees. A freshwater spring had formed a pool; subtle changes had produced a small waterfall and stream which meandered between well-tended lawns. Set on a low hill, the Villa Belucchi held a commanding view of the surrounding countryside.

Guilio Belucchi sat on a wooden seat which was strategically placed so that any user would see the vineyard and buildings that the family owned. Belucchi was of medium height but impressive in body. Square of shoulder and solidly built, he carried no fat. He was ruggedly handsome, his eyes a rich brown topped by bushy eyebrows, his nose big and flattish, his fleshy lips seemingly always poised to smile. At the age of fifty-four he had a healthy crop of hair, it was grey now but gave him a distinguished look. His wife Sophia and the children would be indoors where it was cool. Guilio was in reflective mood, he always came to this quiet place to relax and ponder.

Born to Roberto and Rosa in 1891, Guilio Belucchi was raised in the Chianti region south of Florence. His formative years were spent learning to read and write and the intricacies of the wine business. Under the direction of his father he developed the art of nurturing the vines which would produce the purple grapes from which, in turn, would come the now famous red wine. He was taught wine production from fermentation right through to bottling and final distribution.

Roberto employed fourteen people from a nearby village, a mixture of both men and women. He treated them well and in return they gave hard work, loyalty and friendship. It was not uncommon to see Roberto in the village drinking, gossiping, playing cards or draughts with his workers.

Guilio carried two images of his father in his mind – the thin, tanned face bearing a moustache, his brown eyes shielded from the sun by a tattered old cap, his shirt with the sleeves rolled up was always worn with a waistcoat and he was never without his watch and chain in his pocket. He wore baggy old trousers and a pair of dirty boots with thick string for laces. For weddings, funerals, festivities and business the other Roberto appeared – the one with a collar and tie, the dark suit, highly-polished shoes and, his crowning glory, a bowler hat presented to him by his father. He encouraged Rosa to wear brightly coloured dresses and fussed over the appearance of his children.

Occasionally he made his way to a rickety old garage at the side of the villa. A smile played across his lips as he pretended not to notice Guilio and his sister Lina peering round the corner of a building in anticipation. He would start the engine of a battered old Fiat saloon and ease it out into the yard. The children would squeal with delight and run toward the motor. At this juncture Rosa would appear carrying a wicker basket. To the children this meant a little time spent in the great city of Florence, while their father did some business, followed by a picnic on the banks of the river Arno.

Roberto and Rosa watched their children grow into adults. Guilio mastered the business accounts and maintained the links with customers forged over the years. He then travelled to Rome where he contacted men of ambition and outlined a system where several vineyards would combine and production and employment improved. Initially Roberto had rejected such an idea, his way of life had not changed and he saw no reason why it should now. He eventually settled to listen to Guilio's scheme in detail and then shrugged his shoulders.

"Perhaps we should move on, where did you get the idea anyway?"

"From Marcello Rinaldi."

"I see," Roberto said, quietly.

On a clear day a castle could be seen from the Belucchi property. Set on a hill it belonged to the Rinaldi family. Opulent, their riches were based on jewellery. Five generations had passed since Luigi Rinaldi had sat in a grubby little shop in Naples plying his craft. He had eked out a meagre living for his family for some years but a slice of luck came his way. He produced a beautiful necklace from scraps of gold he found in various parts of the shop. He displayed it and a lady of obvious class stopped to admire his creations. Wife of banker Emilio Vascari, Gina bought the necklace, promising to return to see more of Luigi's work. From that day forward Luigi Rinaldi prospered. Emilio became his patron and business advisor. Luigi moved to new premises, which were more central and well positioned as a customer catchment area. He wore more suits these days, met other businessmen and made contacts. He learned new production techniques and took on two apprentices. All went well and when Emilio suggested another shop open in Rome Luigi was surprised but decided to ride his luck... it did not fail him! Later he bought premises in Florence situated on the famous Ponti Vecchio Bridge. Luigi considered this the pinnacle of his personal achievement. At his death he left a legacy of wealth, a widow, three children and a sound business.

Marcello Rinaldi and Guilio Belucchi had been born within months of each other. Marcello was well educated, used to living in style, enjoying good food and riding his horses around the countryside. He purchased his wine from Roberto but that was as far as any relationship went. At the age of twenty-one Marcello married Graziella Bettega, a society beauty from Rome. Their union produced a son, Gino. Graziella did not enjoy her lifestyle; she missed the parties and pleasures of society membership in Rome. She voiced her regret at moving to the countryside and eventually left to return to her former environment leaving Gino with his father. Marcello was not alone for long, his wealth made him a natural target for female interest. He chose a Florentine girl, Natalia Carracci. She was attractive and quickly settled into the Rinaldi household. She was pregnant when Marcello went to fight in the First World War. He became an officer while Guilio served in the ranks. Both men survived the rigours of war and returned to find that few things had changed. Natalia had persuaded an established jeweller to help her with business and she was raising two sons, Gino and Frederico. Normality returned to the two families but outside their world movement was afoot. A son of a blacksmith, Benito Mussolini, was about to introduce the word Fascist to the Italian language and its tentacles would reach far and wide. A former schoolteacher and journalist, Mussolini would eventually form a totalitarian, single-party regime. Many landowners supported him and black-shirted militia filtered into the countryside to expand their influence. Marcello Rinaldi welcomed fascism and gave both vocal and monetary aid to the cause. The Belucchi family tended to avoid any intervention into their lives, quite content to carry on undisturbed. With the spread of fascism came success for Mussolini, he became dictator of Italy.

Changes were made in Italy but the Belucchi vineyards prospered. Roberto sat in the sun more often. Guilio controlled the business but was not averse to rolling up his sleeves and toiling along with the other employees. Much to the pleasure of his parents he took Sophia Monte as his bride. She was local, slim, pretty and intelligent and Guilio counted himself fortunate to have gained such a prize. Over the next two years Roberto and Rosa gained two grandchildren, Enrico and Claudia. Guilio formed a co-operative scheme with other vineyard owners and, begrudgingly, Roberto had to agree that it was successful. Sophia could play the piano and often the Belucchi villa rang with music and singing. Guilio attained high status in the community and became active in encouraging harmony between all the local people whatever their profession. Because of his happy family life Guilio was content and he took his pleasures where they could be found. The children attended the local school, Enrico appeared ready to follow in his father's footsteps.

The years rolled by. Lina, in her late twenties, married a local butcher. This was a most joyous occasion, the wedding ceremony was carried out in customary fashion and a nearby plaza commandeered for the celebrations. Long tables weighed down with food and drink awaited guests and villagers alike. Sophia's piano had been transported by lorry and, accompanied by a violin, guitar and accordion, she set music and dancing in motion. Roberto and Rosa sat talking to the elderly guests but at one point Lina dragged her father up to dance. He put up a mild protestation but joined in, acquitting himself well for his age and earning applause for his efforts. The tempo of the music gradually quickened and soon the younger element were whirling around the dance area in a wild splash of colour. The village buildings reverberated with sound, gaiety and laughter, the day would stay in the memory for quite a while and would surface fully when Lina announced her first pregnancy twelve months later.

The seasons prevailed, the winters mild with some sun and the heat of the summer cooled by winds from the Mediterranean sea providing ideal conditions for the Belucchi vineyards. Meanwhile Marcello Rinaldi strengthened his ties with Mussolini's fascist regime. His financial aid was soon noticed. He met party hierarchy, throwing his home open for both conferences and parties. Traffic in the area noticeably increased, their occupants mainly stern-looking men in suits. The local population kept their distance, unaware that disruption of their lives was imminent. The heel of Hitler's Germany was applying its military might to parts of Europe. Mussolini envisioned an alliance with Germany to be advantageous in many ways; Italy became part of the Axis forces. German dignitaries now found their way to the Rinaldi castle where they received encouragement and praise.

Guilio was out in the vineyard. He had just picked up a handful of dry soil; he let it run through his fingers. At that moment he saw a cloud of dust rising rapidly from the track on approach toward the villa. Beneath it was a black car containing four men. Guilio had a sense of foreboding and hurried home, he was some distance away. The car was gone when Guilio reached the villa. On entering he heard sobbing, he made his way to its source. He found Rosa crying and Roberto sat close by. There was blood on his head and Sophia was carefully cleaning the wound.

"What happened?"

"Four men came, they said they wished to talk to Father," Sophia said, "They all went into the kitchen, it was quiet at first then we heard shouting and then a sound as if furniture was being knocked over, anyway the four men came out and went to the car and drove away, we found Father on the floor."

Guilio knelt down in front of Roberto.

"What did they want, Father?"

Roberto, obviously shaken, looked at his son.

"They want to use part of our vineyard as an airfield."

"And you objected?"

Roberto nodded.

"I see, can we stop them?"

Roberto, full of despair, said, "No!"

The once quiet countryside was now subjected to the clamour and dust of building. Distraught villagers watched as buildings and vines were destroyed, many men clenched their fists and took a step towards the butchery; they were immediately restrained by their companions. The work was under armed guard by both Italian and German troops and continued unabated. Marcello Rinaldi was blamed for the assault on the local way of life. He stopped acquiring his wine from the Belucchis and bought all his supplies in Florence. He used his position to his advantage – he received an undertaking that his sons would not serve in the armed forces, subsequently Gino became a medical student at the University of Naples and Frederico continued his work in the jewellery trade. There would be no concession of this nature for young Enrico Belucchi but Guilio was determined that his son would not be dragged into the war. A family discussion took place and decisions made. The following afternoon a dilapidated, ancient Fiat saloon chugged its way painfully into the Apennine mountain range. Eventually Guilio stopped the vehicle on a bridge which traversed a ravine. Three young men stepped from the car and for a moment gazed at the scene. Water roared beneath them, foaming white as it dashed against rocks. The riverside was wholly forest, the sun shining down creating a cacophony of different hues among the leaves. Guilio broke the reverie, "Time to go, boys!" Two village youngsters silently shook his hand and Enrico embraced him.

"Goodbye, Father."

"Goodbye son, look after yourself."

Guilio watched as the trio climbed away from him. At the first rise Enrico turned and waved. Guilio raised his hand. Enrico was gone. Guilio stood for a few seconds then shook his head, straightened his shoulders and moved to the Fiat. It would be four years before he saw his son again but messages by word of mouth from the mountains regularly assured the Belucchi family that all was well.

Marcello Rinaldi continued to prosper. His relationship with the authorities brought rewards. The Germans in particular liked to present him with paintings, so much so that he had part of the castle converted into a gallery. He was told that the gifts were valuable but he never asked where they came from. Gino flourished at university, his instructors delighted by his application and dedication to his medical studies prophesying that a dazzling career awaited him. Frederico did not disappoint his father. Although a world war was in progress the Rinaldi jeweller's sales maintained high levels; once again Marcello had used his power, none of his craftsmen had been called upon to wield a rifle. Marcello held parties, regularly inviting staff from the airfield, providing food, drink and entertainment. Guilio and his fellow countrymen tended their individual businesses, the only disturbance coming from the noise of incoming and outgoing aircraft. This pattern of life lasted for some time but it was not to be sustained. News came of a string of military defeats; the tide of war had turned against the Axis drive for world domination. Marcello became isolated, the castle descended into silence. He and Natalia only ventured out for fresh air under cover of darkness, a trusted member of staff fetched supplies from Florence. Airfield movement subsided; no lights were to be seen at night. News circulated that Allied forces were on Italian soil. German soldiers moved south to stem attacks; the airfield was abandoned, left to the mercy of Mother Nature. In the surrounding gloom one bright light shone for Marcello Rinaldi, Gino was to become a surgeon. His success was celebrated quietly, two glasses of wine raised in a toast.

Roberto Belucchi never really recovered from his beating by the fascists. The shock had taken the heart from him, the end came and was expected. Guilio had watched his father's decline; attempts to brighten his days failed, the enforced exile of Enrico was of little help. It came as no surprise when, a year later, Rosa followed her husband. Sorrow and anger was not confined to the Belucchi villa, many of the local population owed their living to the family.

Marcello coughed, and then came awake. He could smell smoke and sensed immediate danger. Quickly he roused Natalia and they both donned dressing gowns and slippers over their night attire before leaving the room. One end of a corridor was well ablaze. Marcello led his wife to the opposite end of the corridor, down a flight of stairs, across the kitchen and out into the open. They ran a long way before breathlessly turning to view the scene. Flames shot high into the air as they consumed the building. The Rinaldis stood and watched, helpless to prevent the disaster. Natalia turned and buried her head in Marcello's chest as the roof collapsed in a cascade of sparks. He turned and as light from the flames penetrated the darkness he could make out the figures of people standing silently in groups. Dozens of eyes were watching the inferno and in that instant he knew that the destruction before him was no accident, he also knew that this was a way of cleansing the countryside of fascism and its representative, himself. The flames died down, he and Natalia were at the mercy of the crowd. It was then that an old Fiat car came up to them. Guilio Belucchi leaned over and opened the door.

"Get in."

Marcello glanced briefly at the castle before helping Natalia into the motor.

"Thank you… Guilio."

"Don't thank me, I won't allow my people to have your blood on their hands."

He set the car in motion, heading for Florence.

Part Seven

CONSPIRACIES

The war had come and gone, leaving the people of Florence to clear away the destruction, both material and human. Most of the important buildings had survived but new bridges would have to be constructed across the River Arno.

Surgeon Gino Rinaldi, dedicated to his work, had treated Italian, British and German patients. Not until the flood of humanity through his operating theatre eased did he notice that nurse Maria Cantello was not only highly efficient at her job but very pretty. She was slim with long dark hair tucked under her cap, her eyes a deep brown; she was the daughter of a local businessman. Cautious questioning by Gino revealed that Maria had no male attachments. Ever bold, he invited her out to dinner, she accepted and their courtship began. The relationship blossomed and acquaintances and friends were in no way surprised when the pair announced their intent to wed.

No expense was spared for the wedding. The Rinaldi and Cantello households shared the cost. Dress was formal, the ceremony conducted by a bishop in a local church and a sizeable hall hired for the reception. A sumptuous sit-down meal was provided, despite enforced food shortages, and the music provided by a band selected by the bride. As the party warmed up and the noise level increased Gino chose a moment to speak to his father, Marcello.

"Can we have a word in private?"

"Of course, Gino."

The men located an empty room.

"What is it, Gino?"

"I need cash, I can get a large supply of drugs from England to help build a practice here in Florence."

Marcello said, "Who's the supplier?"

"An Englishman, I gave him some new legs a few months back."

"I see, and how is this consignment coming?"

"By air, unofficially."

"Which airfield do you propose to use?"

"The one on Guilio Belucchi's land."

Marcello stroked his chin thoughtfully for a few seconds then quickly strode to the door and opened it, checking that there was no one in close proximity. Satisfied, he closed the door.

"There are paintings and art treasures at the castle, they are worth a small fortune, I believe."

Gino's eyes opened in surprise, "But the gallery was burnt down!"

Marcello smiled, "That's true but I emptied it when Mussolini fell, Natalia and I became very vulnerable and I was in no position to protect our property."

"So where is the stuff?"

"Under the dining room floor in boxes."

"Who else knows about this, Father?"

"Eight German soldiers."

"And they're running back to Germany… or dead!"

"Correct."

Gino smiled, "Perfect, now we can arrange a swap – drugs for art using just one round trip."

It was Marcello's turn to smile, "We'll need two vehicles for the move, four men can handle the lifting; contact your man in England, Gino."

* * * * *

David Collins read the letter then passed it to Des Hilton.

"What do you think?"

Hilton took his time before answering, "I think we have to trust your Italian surgeon, David, but do we have enough buyers for the merchandise?"

"I have a few collectors but Phillip has a much bigger market, I don't see a problem."

"Shall I speak to him?"

"Yes, Des."

Phillip replaced the receiver on its cradle and settled back in his chair. He was being asked to take a risk with unseen goods, but so was David, he thought. Reaching a decision he made a quick telephone call to Des Hilton before making a longer one to Group Captain Geoff Arnold.

* * * * *

Guilio Belucchi watched as the telltale dustcloud approached the villa. The big, shiny car stopped and the driver got out. Guilio's eyes narrowed when he saw who it was.

"Good afternoon, Mister Belucchi."

Guilio stood up. "Gino Rinaldi, no less, and what may I ask is the purpose of your visit?"

"I would like to use your airfield for one night."

"Oh! Clandestine flying is it?"

"Yes."

"Well you're very frank, what cargo and where from?"

"Drugs from England, to set me up in practice in Florence."

"What's wrong with the official route?"

"Length of time, red tape and cost."

"All this for the good of the people… and Gino Rinaldi!"

Gino ignored the jibe.

"We wouldn't expect this favour for nothing."

Guilio chuckled and then looked into Gino's eyes, thinking.

"When?"

"One week from today."

"You have a very attractive wife, Mister Rinaldi, seven nights from now she comes to a hotel of my choice in Florence. Gino hesitated, his face reddening. Slowly he recovered his poise, he produced a business card, handing it to Guilio.

"Call me with the arrangement."

Guilio flicked his forehead with the index finger of his right hand, "Don't worry, I will," he said.

Gino turned abruptly and strode to the car, slamming the door as he took his seat. Guilio looked at the card then slipped it into his shirt pocket, his smile was mirthless as he listened to the car roar away down the track.

* * * * *

Messages passed between Birmingham, Worcester, Florence and Paris. André Dupont had selected an unused airfield in a remote part of France where Arnold would land to refuel the aircraft. Loaded onto the barge in darkness, the drug consignment travelled from Birmingham to Worcester in daylight, everyone concerned was relieved when it had arrived and was locked in David Collins' yard aboard a large van ready for the next phase.

The fox padded through his territory. The night was cold, there was frost on his breath. He was on his way home, a rabbit and a few insects had provided a good meal. He had almost reached the concrete strip when his ears caught an unusual sound. It grew louder and twin lights split the darkness, the fox drew back into cover. Men and lights moved about and there was conversation then, for a time, all the lights were extinguished. More sounds came, this time from the sky. As one, the lights were switched on again, the fox cowered lower, curiosity preventing him from running away. The noise level soared and a huge machine came and landed on the concrete strip, propellers twirling. Animals scurried for cover, afraid of this intruder into their domain, the fox however, stayed where he was. Speed and timing were essential, little time was wasted on ceremony, the van was backed up to the aircraft, its load quickly transferred by all available hands. Doors closed, cargo secured, Geoff Arnold set the aircraft moving again, the engines rising to a crescendo as it sped down the runway before climbing away into the night. The men on the ground swiftly boarded their vehicle and left the airfield. Peace returned to the land, its creatures ventured forth and the fox rose from the grass and loped off to its lair.

* * * * *

Guilio Belucchi had told Enrico about the Rinaldi arrangement, leaving out the part alluding to Maria. Enrico had protested loudly but quietened when Guilio pointed out that the Rinaldis would now be in their debt. The day arrived, the Belucchis and their employees were out in the vineyards, it was one of these who told Guilio that there was movement at the castle. Guilio glanced at Enrico and together they headed for the ruined building. Overgrown bushes provided ample cover and the Belucchis were soon well positioned to watch any activity. Four men, including Marcello and Gino, were using shovels to remove ash that covered the floor of the former dining room. Gradually all the floorboards were exposed. Marcello pointed, a crowbar was inserted and a floorboard lifted clear. Guilio and Enrico exchanged looks and saw the entire floor raised and moved to one side to reveal a number of boxes beneath. Two lorries were backed up to the site and the men carefully lifted the boxes onto them. Eventually, their task at the castle finished, the men departed.

"What was all that, Father?"

"Ill-gotten gains from Mussolini and the Germans, no doubt," Guilio said.

"And these will be going to England?"

"Yes, you can watch if you wish, I will be busy in Florence."

"Oh?"

"Yes, I have a business appointment."

Used to the noise of aircraft the population around the Villa Belucchi slept on as, once again, Geoff Arnold brought the Dakota in to land. He fretted a little when he saw the onload but there were no interruptions and he relaxed once he was airborne for France and home where he would, for a second time, disrupt the life of the fox and his fellow creatures. Earlier, in a hotel room in Florence Guilio, shirt open, had gazed in anticipation as Maria Rinaldi, a half-smile on her lips, began to unbutton her blouse...

* * * * *

Only one room was lit in the antique shop. Collins, Hilton and the Simmonds brothers were celebrating, champagne was flowing freely. During the day the boxes from Italy had been opened. Des Hilton had spent some hours inspecting paintings and art treasures and had taken photographs of each item. He told Collins that Gino Rinaldi had honoured his obligations and, after deductions for expenses, that he would at least break even on the deal. Collins, his personal debt to Gino paid in full, reached for his champagne glass.

Mike Simmons said, "Where's Joe?"

"Out on his rounds of course!" said Collins.

"Bit harsh isn't it after his work on the Italian job?"

"Come off it, we've got to make some money, you know."

They all laughed, with the exception of David Collins.

Two sets of photographs were produced and David and Phillip Reardon began their sales campaigns. Collins made a small profit but the bulk of the treasures went to Birmingham and Reardon. Des Hilton went with the barge on this occasion; he talked to Phillip at length before rejoining the Simmons for the return to Worcester.

* * * * *

Marc Dubois woke with the sun on his face. He sat up and looked at his girlfriend Catherine, she was sound asleep. He vacated the bed and put on dressing gown and slippers before making his way to the living room. I'll cook the breakfast, he thought. Humming to himself he threw open the curtains and stretched, utterly relaxed. Instant death came through the window, the bullet entering his forehead. The thud of his body hitting the floor brought Catherine to consciousness. Frowning she, too, got out of bed and sauntered into the living room. Dubois was lying face down on the floor. First she saw the hole in the window then, alarmed, she turned him over. His eyes were open but he could see nothing in this world. Catherine saw the bullet hole in the head and the blood, she screamed… and screamed!

Inspector Bouché looked at the girl. She was still in her dressing gown, her hair was a mess and she chain-smoked.

"How long have you been with Dubois?"

"Three months."

"What did he do for a living?"

"Not a lot, he was always out at meetings, or at least, that's what he said."

"Did he talk about these meetings?"

"No."

At this point a detective of Bouché's team leaned through the door, "Inspector," he said.

Bouché said, "Excuse me."

He was led to the bedroom, floorboards had been taken up.

"What have we got?"

"A rifle, ammunition, documents and a large amount of money."

"And?"

"All the documents relate to overpowering the government in Paris and moving it here to Vichy as it was in the war, we have also found a book with a list of names and addresses."

"Careless!"

"He must have felt safe being at the centre of the old regime."

"Wrap everything up here and take care of the girl."

"Yes, sir."

Bouché strolled towards his car feeling the warmth of the sun on his body. He looked about him. The daily routine of the city was going on uninterrupted. Despite Dubois and his cronies' efforts Vichy would never be the seat of government again. Further arrests were made and, during his investigations, Bouché found that a Louis Dubois had died at the hands of an assassin in Paris a few months earlier... he was Marc Dubois' younger brother! This was a political killing, the gunman has long gone and there will be no trail left to follow, the authorities will see to that, he mused. He tossed the relevant file into the out-tray on his desk.

"Better look at the living miscreants," he said.

* * * * *

Phillip Reardon received a telegram requesting his presence in Paris. He used this excuse to take Valerie and the children for a holiday, having warned his wife about the meeting beforehand.

"Who are you going to see, Phillip?"

"André Dupont, an old friend in French Intelligence."

"Sounds important."

"Could be."

Reardon left the hotel lift and made his way to the room where Dupont waited. He was surprised to find two men sat on either side of the door. They stood up as he approached.

"Mister Reardon?"

"Yes."

"Pardon the intrusion, sir."

Phillip was thoroughly frisked, not for the first time in his life.

"Carry on, sir."

"Thank you."

André Dupont came toward him, hand outstretched.

"Welcome, Phillip, take a seat while I pour a little refreshment. The room has been checked for 'bugs', we can speak freely."

Seated, he came straight to the business in hand.

"A former German general was caught trying to escape from Germany with his family. He was never going to succeed, he was at a border checkpoint and his accent and poor paperwork gave him away. We think he knew that this would happen but he made an attempt to bribe the guards with a list containing names and addresses where stolen paintings and artefacts could be found. My comrades in French intelligence have not seen the list."

"That's because André Dupont has it," interjected Reardon.

"Very smart, Phillip, you know me too well."

"Where do I come in?"

"I require a small team to investigate these locations, this must, of course, contain someone who can check the authenticity of any items found. I neither have the time or resources for the task but you as a trusted friend may be able to help."

Phillip took a large swig of his drink, his mind focused on the proposal before him.

"What is the situation in Germany at the moment, do we know?"

"Most of the addresses are in cities which have been flattened by Allied bombing, the morale and will of the people is extremely low at this time, they are at their most vulnerable but I would advise the team not to look too prosperous. There will be a need for careful reconnaissance before the team moves in."

"Understood," Phillip said, "Presumably we offer to buy the items?"

"No, your group will be our pathfinders, someone else will collect the found items and take care of the custodians."

"Sounds ominous," Phillip commented.

"Fear not, Phillip, the war is over, a new way ahead beckons, no more barbarism, I think everyone has had their fill for now."

"The way ahead, André?"

"A unified Europe, our countries coming together both in trade and harmony."

"I can tell you have a passion for this idea, is it feasible?"

"I believe so, but it will take time and determination to bring to fruition. The men collecting your team's finds will be of mixed nationalities, everything will be returned to its rightful owner."

"And the cost of the operation?" asked Phillip.

"Covered by all European countries concerned, you have to realise that this plan for union has gone well beyond the germ stage."

"I'm impressed."

André refilled the now empty glasses.

"Can you provide the 'pathfinders', Phillip?"

"Gladly, André."

André Dupont's face split into a huge grin. He sat heavily in his chair breathing a sigh of relief.

"I knew it," he said.

"At this moment you look ten years' younger André."

"I feel good, as you see, but there is one more act of barbarism to perform, unfortunately. The next assassination attempt must fail and the sniper's demise must be brought about at the hand of a German."

"Another brick in the European consortium?"

"Precisely," André said, serious again.

* * * * *

Joe Thompson was cold and anxious. It had snowed yesterday and now it had frozen and crunched under his boots as he moved around on the canal towpath. At last he heard rather than saw the barge approach. It was breaking through thin ice as Mike Simmonds brought her smoothly into her berth. Des Hilton had been to visit his parents, travelling with the Simmonds brothers.

Hilton came ashore, "Hi, Joe, are you alright?"

"Yes, it's a bit parky though."

"I suppose David's tucked up warm in bed?"

"No doubt," Joe said, "Let's get the stuff into the van."

Des nodded, "Right."

The four men offloaded the contraband into Joe's vehicle and waved as he pulled away, heading for the Collins yard, there to check everything was correct before commencing his distribution runs. He would be busy for the rest of the day; the next two days he would be out at the farms followed by two days' delivering to those customers on David Collins' list. Margaret knew what he did. She had been shocked at first by the illegal aspect of Joe's job, she gradually accepted the situation but was not totally convinced when she found out that David was involved in the scheme. Everything faded into the background when the contractions started. Margaret remained calm and telephoned her mother. Minutes later Harold and Maureen Collins arrived and they were soon on their way to the local maternity unit.

Joe parked the van, locked the yard gate and walked to the house. He was a little concerned to find his home in darkness. He immediately spotted an envelope propped against a vase on the mantelpiece. He ripped it open feverishly, reading the words quickly. For a moment he panicked and then said, "Slow down, Joe," to himself. He extinguished the light, locked the door and walked back to the yard.

The Sister said, "Good evening, Mister Thompson, your wife is in ward three, go straight in."

"Thank you."

Margaret saw him coming, smiled and held out her arms. Joe clasped her to him, "Are you alright, my love?"

"I'm fine, Joe, meet your baby son!"

Joe looked into the cradle and saw the face and hands of his child. Blue eyes appeared to look at him and gingerly Joe reached to touch the baby's fingers and gazed in wonder as they closed around his own. Joe constantly questioned Margaret's health and stared at his son. Margaret laughed but understood his mood exactly, "I'm afraid he won't be ready to play football this weekend, Joe."

Joe laughed and visibly relaxed.

"We have to find a name for him."

Margaret smiled, "Think about it, then we'll talk about it on your next visit."

"OK."

Five days later Brian Harold Thompson was carried into the outside world. He arrived home to his own bedroom with cot and toys ready. Margaret settled into her role as a mother and allowed Joe to parade Brian in front of relatives and friends for a while then quietly roped him in to change nappies, give Brian his milk and, later, bathe him prior to bedtime.

Maureen began to fuss about, arranging the christening. She had taken charge of proceedings and her husband and daughter let her get on with it.

"Your mother's in her element."

"I know, great isn't it?"

"Keeps her off my back."

"Now, now, Father!"

Harold changed the subject, "Excellent names you chose for the boy."

"We thought you would approve."

Harold opened his trusty wine cabinet, "I think it's time to wet the baby's head."

"What, again?"

Harold winked, "We have to make sure the job's done properly."

Margaret smiled, "Mine's a sherry."

"Right you are," he said.

The christening took place at the Holy Trinity Church. Maureen had made doubly sure that everyone was on time. The service was held straight after Sunday School was over and Maureen was delighted when some of the pupils stayed behind to join in. She laid on food and drink at the Collins' residence. David displayed his charming self, Harold and Margaret exchanged knowing glances but said nothing.

It snowed again, the canal appeared to be frozen solid. Someone threw a brick into the centre of the waterway and it bounced before slithering across to the other side. One or two brave souls then tested the ice, gaining in confidence as they ascertained its firmness and soon the canal was filled with skaters. David Collins' barge was held fast by the ice; he called a meeting at the shop. When they were all seated he said, "I propose to do our next run by road."

Hilton and the Simmonds looked at each other. Des cleared his throat, "We three are going back to Birmingham, David, we have got another job to go to."

"Oh?"

"Phillip Reardon wants us to do a job for him in Germany."

David's face flushed with rage.

"I might've guessed it was him, what does he want you to do?"

"It's a secret, David."

"I suppose that if I had legs I would have been in on this deal too?"

The trio looked awkwardly at each other.

"Probably," Hilton muttered.

"When do you plan on going then?" asked David.

"Today."

David did not hesitate, "Well, goodbye, enjoy yourselves," and wheeled himself away into the confines of a rear office.

The group stood around sheepishly for a few moments then, as one, they trooped out of the shop. They failed to hear a window smash as David hurled a chair through it. He sat in his wheelchair looking around. The place was empty, silent, he could hear himself breathing. He was startled when the telephone rang.

"Hello!"

"Hello, David, it's Phillip Reardon here."

"Oh."

"Listen, I know I've taken your staff away and I want to make amends, I can offer you two men to help out. They are both young, capable and can handle your transport system. Their names are Martin Edwards and John Mooney – are you interested?"

David hesitated a little, "Yes, I have to be."

"Is the barge iced in?"

"At the moment, yes. I will let you know when it's free."

"Right, David, as soon as she's ready call and I will bring the lads to you."

David put the telephone down and felt better but did not relish the fact that Reardon had taken more control of the canal venture.

"You want me to what?" Harold said angrily.

"Return to the shop, Father."

Harold looked at Maureen.

"Why is that, David?"

"Des, Mike and Tony are going to work in Germany for Phillip Reardon."

"So you are on your own?"

"Yes."

Harold noticed hesitancy in his son, he knew he was eating humble pie.

"Anything else, David?"

"I would like Margaret to come back to work part-time and thought mother might babysit for her."

"You've got a damn cheek, son!"

"Yes I know," said David, quietly.

"Leave it, David, we will sort it out," Maureen said.

Harold was not prepared to let the subject drop at this point.

"How much control would I have?"

"Full control as before I came home."

"And where will you be?"

"Running the shop here in St Paul's."

"I see, closer to home, cuts travelling in the wheelchair," said Harold, thoughtfully.

Maureen saw an opportunity to take the heat out of the discussion.

"Sounds reasonable, Harold."

"Umm!" he said, pensively.

Maureen sensed a decline in her husband's anger and when they were alone she used gentle persuasion, coaxing Harold into a better frame of mind and subsequent acceptance of David's proposition. Margaret was amiable with regard to the situation.

"A little extra cash is always handy, when do I start?"

Maureen smiled inwardly, another crisis averted, she thought. David moved into the shop, he needed an office and the present manager, Peter Gough, who lived locally, made space for himself in the shop storeroom. He was a little reluctant but was appeased somewhat when another telephone was installed for him. David contacted Joe and they went round the black market customers telling them about the new arrangement and the need to maintain secrecy if they spoke to Harold. That mission over, David breathed a sigh of relief, two days later the ice melted on the canal, Reardon delivered the new boys and normal business was resumed.

* * * * *

The three men approached the house cautiously, well spread out. The shot brought up a spurt of stones as it ploughed into the ground close to Mike Simmond's foot; the trio melted into available cover. Des Hilton called out in German.

"Hello, we are friends."

"What do you want?" it was a female voice.

"We bring you help."

There was a long pause.

"Come on up… slowly!"

The men did as they were bid. They found themselves faced by the woman. She had long, unkempt hair, a thin face, blue eyes shifting nervously from man to man as they moved in. She held a double-barrelled shotgun, pointing it at Des Hilton. A little girl was clinging to her shabby dress, a thumb in her mouth. A boy, older, stood to one side silent, watching.

"You are Annette Keller wife of Colonel Friedrich Keller?"

"I was, he went to the Russian front, he never returned."

"I'm sorry to hear that, we understand that he brought some art treasures home for storage."

The shotgun wavered, but only for an instant.

"So?"

"They were stolen and the owners want them returned but there is a payment made to anyone who has been carrying out 'custodial' duties … shall we say?"

The woman lowered the shotgun and walked slowly towards the house, Des nodded and the rest of the group followed her. Annette Keller brought a key from the house and approached what had been a garage; its double doors had been painted green but it was peeling badly, Hilton noted that the padlock looked quite new. The men swung the doors open to be faced with a neat stack of packages and boxes of all shapes and sizes.

Des turned to the woman, "We would like to inspect these items."

"And if it's what you are looking for?"

"A team of men will come in with vehicles to get the consignment and you will be paid accordingly."

"On one condition," the woman said.

"And what's that?"

"You come with them."

Hilton paused, "Agreed," he said.

The Simmonds brothers opened the packages for Des. The work took a little over three hours punctuated only when the boy brought some bread, schnitzel and a bottle of schnapps. Des thanked him and the boy turned away without speaking. Later Hilton stood up, his job completed for now.

"Well?" asked Mike.

"Worth a fortune."

The brothers smiled. "Good," Tony uttered.

Dusk was falling; Des went to find Annette Keller.

"Lock the garage up, I will return tomorrow." She nodded.

Re-packaged, the artefacts were carefully loaded aboard two vehicles. Hilton was present while a German diplomat spoke to Annette Keller and paid her what appeared to be quite a generous sum of money. She looked at Des Hilton and he read the gratitude in her eyes.

He said "All finished?"

The man shook the woman's hand, "All done," he said.

Hilton and Annette exchanged looks.

"Goodbye, Mrs Keller."

"Goodbye and thank you."

Des went to climb into the cab of the lorry but something made him pause. He looked back up the hill and saw the solitary figure of the boy looking down at him. Des waved and was pleasantly surprised when the boy responded with a wave of his own. Hilton sat back, there would be many places to visit over the next months, not all of them safe, he thought.

* * * * *

André Dupont cleared his desk; he liked to leave his office tidy. He made sure everything was secure before leaving for his apartment. He looked at this watch; it was just after five o'clock. André grunted quietly with satisfaction. He enjoyed the working hours, not at all like the old days in intelligence when he used to spend his days with eyes red-rimmed from lack of sleep. The new post and title of European Advisor appealed to him and his enthusiasm for the task surprised even him. One wall of his office was home to a large map of Europe and he spent a great amount of time reading literature about the history and culture of the countries expected to join the envisaged organisation. The outstanding problem for the whole exercise was lack of finance following the war but this was solved when the United States of America provided necessary aid. Countless meetings took place in a conference room close to Dupont's office. All aspects of European integration were discussed here but it was also the place where he noticed an attractive lady. Oval of face, hazel-eyed with long auburn hair, Celine Rochelle was tall, slim and elegant. It was during some discussion, which seemed irrelevant to the business in hand, when Dupont's eyes began to wander around the assembled group. He found Madame Rochelle looking directly at him. Her eyes twinkled and a smile played around her lips. Dupont imperceptibly nodded, folded his arms and acted as if he was deeply interested in the speaker's rhetoric. He stole a glance at Celine, her hand was covering her mouth in a massive attempt to suppress uncontrolled laughter. Finally the meeting ended and Dupont moved quickly to intercept Celine Rochelle's departure.

"Would you care to enjoy a glass of wine in my office, Madame?"

There was a minimal hesitation, as seemed appropriate.

"Why yes, thank you, Mister Dupont."

"André."

"Right… André."

Seated, Celine asked for red wine and noted his steady, controlled movements. They immediately found conversation easy. He had seen a wedding ring on her finger and she saw the direction of his gaze, she smiled.

"I'm a widow, André – my husband Ferdinand was killed by the Boche two years ago."

"I'm sorry, I didn't mean to…"

"It's alright, André, I can live with it now."

They both relaxed.

"Where did you serve in the war André?"

"All over Europe and Africa, I was with intelligence."

"I see, so this job is a complete change for you."

"Yes, I can enjoy Paris to the full again."

"You were born here?"

"Yes."

"So was I, being a Public Relations Officer based near home suits me fine."

"Would you dine with me this evening, Celine?"

"Yes, André, I will."

André chose his favourite restaurant and Celine appeared pleased with the cuisine. They talked freely about themselves. They both spoke English and German, useful assets in their common goal, Celine had to travel occasionally with her superiors and André missed her presence. She re-introduced him to Paris, pointing out the places of interest from the top of the Eiffel Tower. They visited the Louvre museum, the Bastille, Notre Dame and many other Paris attractions. He took her to race meetings at Longchamps and watched her animation when a horse she had bet on won or came close to it. Like most Parisians André and Celine found great pleasure in pavement cafes where they sat to enjoy warmth, coffee and the sight of the world going by. They would laze around on the banks of the River Seine, Celine would sit back and take in the scenery as André displayed his prowess in a rowing boat. She, in turn, taught him to appreciate opera. André met her few relatives and she his; he introduced her to Phillip Reardon and his family when they visited Paris, André was amused when Celine ambushed Phillip and led him into a lengthy discussion regarding the English view of a unified Europe.

When they were alone André said, "Well?"

"Well what?"

"How did Phillip react to your probing?"

Celine sniffed, "He was non-committal!"

André laughed, ducking her feigned punch. The combination of their work and leisure hours together began to lead Celine and André into a relationship that could go deeper than friendship. He was sure that there was a romance developing between them but, so far, he had held back from any physical approach in respect for Celine's dead husband, if there was to be a future for them she would have to make the first move.

* * * * *

Paul Parker stretched pleasurably into wakefulness. The bed beside him was empty and the aroma of coffee penetrated his nostrils, he sat up. His current girlfriend Marilyn Cooper, a petite blonde, was on the balcony looking out over the

London landscape. She hardly moved as his arms encircled her and he kissed her neck.

"Morning, Marilyn."

"Good morning, Mister Parker," she said brightly.

He looked up, "Nice day."

"Yes, let's go eat," Marilyn said, gently breaking his grip.

They had met at a party there some months earlier, introduced by one of Paul's former girlfriends. Their feelings for each other had blossomed and Marilyn had quickly agreed to move into his apartment. She worked as a secretary in central London and Paul told her that he had inherited money and travelled occasionally. Living together had lost them many friends, and neighbours treated them as lepers but they were happy together and did their best to ignore prejudice.

The letter came as no surprise to Paul, he hid it until Marilyn had gone to work before opening it. A photograph of a young man dropped onto the table in front of him, Paul studied the features. Full instructions were handwritten on the reverse of the photograph. Twenty-four hours later Paul boarded an Arnold Airways Dakota travelling from London Airport to Tempelhof, Berlin. The German capital was heavily damaged but a small diagram pointed him in the right direction. He found lodgings and immediately set out to reconnoitre the proposed killing ground; he was unimpressed with what he saw. The target was scheduled to attend some kind of meeting in a building which was partially damaged. The only vantage point for Parker was a ruined building one hundred yards away; the area around it had been cleared of rubble. Paul approached the ruin from the rear. There were stairs available but escape would be difficult, surprise and ensuing confusion would be his only cover. He made a longer than usual inspection of the site before departing, unaware that his every move was watched by a man who was some distance away using binoculars.

Wilhelm Brecht was a rising political star in Germany, his vision of Europe running parallel with that of André Dupont although they had never met. He had expressed doubts with regard to the venue for today's meeting but was persuaded that as its theme would be about his country rising from destruction the physical background would give force to his message. He was further encouraged by the attendance and security. Many people had travelled to listen to him, they had realised a great potential in the young idealist. Following introductions to various dignitaries, Brecht stepped onto a newly-constructed stage and launched into his speech balanced with both quiet and fiery rhetoric. He received a long ovation at the end and many people came forward to shake him by the hand.

Peter Mueller, former sergeant in the army was now Head of Security in a large section of Berlin. Today was special; his task was to protect Wilhelm Brecht. Word had filtered through to his headquarters that an assassination attempt would take place. Accordingly Mueller had positioned his men to watch the location and he was now in possession of a description of a suspect. He practised shooting with pistol and rifle on a regular basis and had assumed full responsibility for this operation. He was positioned in a window above the meeting place, keeping out of sight but alert for word coming through on his radio. It crackled into life, the quarry had been spotted, case in hand, entering the nearby bomb-blasted former apartment building.

Paul Parker peered through the aperture, which had once been a window, quickly appraising the scene before him. Smoothly he assembled his rifle and then surveyed the area again through the telescopic sight; satisfied, he awaited developments.

Peter Mueller saw movement in the ruin opposite. His man in the field pinpointed, Mueller played the waiting game, as did his adversary.

Wilhelm Brecht stepped out into a Berlin overcast by grey clouds, rain threatening, he headed for his car. His would-be killer loaded a bullet into his weapon and eased himself into the required firing position. Absolute concentration took over; Parker selected his target through his sight, his finger seeking and finding the trigger. Perfectly still, Parker prepared to release the deadly missile; an instant later he was falling away from the window, blood spurting from the back of his head. Peter Mueller waited, he was certain of a hit but caution had seen him reach the end of the war with but a few scratches. He glanced down, the only sign of disturbance was thunder on the distant horizon. He left the building by a rear exit and made his way in a wide circle finishing behind the sniper's location. He waved two men from their hiding places, led them into the building and began, slowly, to climb the stairs. The silence was eerie and fragments of glass crunched beneath their feet making an undetected approach virtually impossible. Mueller steeled himself for some movement above him, but it never came. They found Paul Parker lying on his back, his eyes staring blankly at the ceiling. The hole in his forehead bore testimony to Mueller's marksmanship. He bent down and closed the gunman's eyes thinking, I've done this before. He saw the rifle, picked it up, checked it, and then put it into his shoulder aiming it into the air. He looked at his colleagues.

"What a beautiful piece of equipment this is. Get this mess cleared away and remember, this man never existed!"

Mueller left the building unaware that he had avenged the death of his former officer Von Frober; Brecht was gone, unaware how close he had come to death. The next day, in his office, André Dupont read a message delivered by special courier. He allowed himself a sigh of relief, placed the paper in an ashtray and put a match to it. He opened a desk drawer and took out a bottle of cognac and a glass, his nerves returned to their normally unruffled condition.

* * * * *

The art recovery team had made good progress in its venture. Many valuable artefacts had been returned to their rightful owners. They had faced one near-disaster, Tony Simmonds had knocked on a particular front door and a bullet had been fired through it. Tony had fallen and Hilton and Mike Simmonds had dragged him into cover and inspected the damage. There was a lot of blood but, fortunately, the injury was a flesh wound in the upper arm. Hilton had called in local police who had surrounded the property; they had subsequently flushed out a former infantry officer, his cache of art treasures was quite considerable, now the team was on its way to Berlin.

Des used the door-knocker and stepped to one side, no bullet this time! The house was large. Situated in what had once been a fashionable, tree-lined street, it had suffered bomb damage as had everything around it. Some seconds elapsed before the door opened to reveal a tall woman dressed in black, a white lace shawl draped around her shoulders. Her brown hair was groomed and her oval face portrayed a striking, if somewhat, faded beauty, her eyes were a remarkably clear blue. The men before her were stopped in their tracks. Des Hilton recovered first and cleared his throat.

"Good morning, are you Mrs Frieda Hoffmann wife of Colonel Heinz Hoffman?"

"I am; how may I help?" The voice was steady, cultivated.

"We understand your husband has a number of paintings and art treasures in his possession."

Frieda Hoffmann opened the door wider and waved them inside.

"Please come in, gentlemen."

She led them down a long hallway. Hilton noted the tiled flooring, carved wooden ceiling and statues, signs of real opulence. They were led into a room which was totally undamaged. Hilton surveyed the decor, the furniture and heavy curtains; there was a well-stocked bookcase, and a clutch of glasses and a full decanter on the table.

"May I offer you all a drink? At least the bombs failed to reach the cellar."

Hilton watched her pour red wine, her hands were rough, her nails dirty. They all picked up their glasses and Hilton introduced himself and his colleagues and outlined the purpose of their visit in detail. Frieda listened to him and put down her glass.

"The treasures you seek are in the cellar along with the wine, they are not only beautiful but probably very valuable – Heinz knew good things when he saw them."

The trio left the house after Des had completed his inspection of the items in question. As they moved away Mike said, "Well?"

Hilton smiled, "Colonel Hoffmann definitely knew what to look for."

Tony said, "Are we talking about the art or the woman, Des?"

"Both," he said.

Des Hilton supervised the removal of the art treasures from the Hoffmann cellar.

"Have you been a widow long, Mrs Hoffmann?"

"Please call me Frieda."

"Desmond… most people simply call me Des."

"Right, Des it is, my husband was killed in Florence."

"Oh!"

"The way you said that – does it mean something?"

"I was there."

"I see, how coincidental."

"Frieda… would you dine with me this evening?"

"Where?"

"We are living in a hotel, the food is quite good, only the choice is limited, of course."

"Yes, I will look forward to it."

"Good, I will be here around eight o'clock."

"I'll be ready."

Hilton was humming a tune as he climbed into the lorry, Frieda was in the doorway; he waved. Later the Simmonds brothers lingered in the hotel bar while their leader entertained Frieda Hoffmann. Their conversation was light but Des noticed her hands again, the nails were clean, she followed his scrutiny.

She laughed, "I'm a 'rubble woman'."

"A what?"

"A 'rubble woman', if you come around the city tomorrow you will see hundreds of us shifting piles of rubbish into lorries as they follow us."

"It sounds a great idea, you don't mind?"

"Not at all, Des, sometimes my back complains but I can live with that."

To Des the evening appeared to go well, he was further encouraged when Frieda allowed him to kiss her before entering her domain. The following day he watched the 'rubble women' at work, they were akin to ants and the lorries were constantly on the move. Eventually Hilton's patience was rewarded, he managed to find Frieda despite the rough clothes, her headscarf and a film of dust covering her face. After a quick conversation he left satisfied... he had another date!

* * * * *

Valerie Reardon prepared dinner. She had farmed the children out to their grandparents. André Dupont was coming to see Phillip, neither of them knew why although he suspected Europe came somewhere in the scheme of things. André duly arrived and enjoyed a drink and looked at framed photographs of the children.

"You have it all, Phillip – two great looking children and a beautiful wife, what more could you want?"

Valerie caught his words, she beamed, suddenly the food took on a new importance, it had to be perfect, she thought. Dinner went according to plan, André expressed his thanks and he and Phillip cleared the dining table and washed up. Valerie made a tactful withdrawal, her father's house was within walking distance. Replenished glass in hand, Dupont came straight to the point of his visit.

"I want you to work on the European project with me in Paris."

"You mean live in Paris, André?"

"Precisely."

"House, Valerie, children's education?"

"I see the persuasion of Valerie to move as the only real problem, everything else is easily taken care of."

"Easy for you to say and what will the job entail?"

"All aspects of Europe integration with special regard to membership of the United Kingdom."

"Travel?"

"Some, but not like the old days."

"Office?"

"Ready and waiting."

"You have it all tied up, André."

"You could say that," said Dupont, smugly.

* * * * *

Word soon travelled round the Birmingham criminal underground that a black market 'baron' wanted to get rid of his business. Two parties showed interest but this was soon reduced to one when a little muscle was applied in the right places. Jack 'Scarface' Wilkins ruled his empire with an iron fist. He attended the same school as Mike and Tony Simmonds but had passed through its portals two years after them. The Wilkins family had a bad reputation. All the males and one or two of the females had tasted prison life, Jack had been to borstal for assaulting a cousin. He was never perturbed when using some arm-twisting to achieve his evil ends, people in the know avoided the Wilkins' domain like the plague. Jack himself was stocky, he had a round head, small, penetrating eyes and his hair was permanently crew-cut in style; he always wore black clothing, he imagined it intimidated people. Over the years he had developed a not too detailed knowledge of the law. His early business in the world of crime had been financed by his forebears who had fallen foul of the law; Jack had vowed that his one period spent inside would be his last. He indulged in petty crime for a short time, but a successful Post Office robbery which involved him and three other men yielded a much better reward than expected. Encouraged, Jack and his 'gang' carried out more thefts, mostly nocturnal, but eyes were upon him! Local gangland boss Eric Wilde saw Wilkins as an intruder and possible threat to the stability of this hard-earned territory.

So it was that one evening when Jack was making a beeline for his local pub he found himself being bundled into a slowly moving car. He struggled initially but soon found that resistance was fruitless. His three captors looked tough and businesslike and were soon ushering him up a flight of stairs into a large room. He was immediately faced by a big desk; behind it sat a man whom Jack took to be elderly. Wilde was sixty years old, thin-faced and grey-haired but he emanated an aura of power, his eyes steady and unblinking as he surveyed his reluctant guest.

"Take a seat, Mister Wilkins," he gestured.

Jack took the proffered chair sensing one of his kidnappers move in close behind him.

"I am Eric Wilde, we have been watching your exploits very closely Jack... I may call you Jack?"

"Yes..."

"Mister Wilde, Jack... Yes, Mister Wilde!"

"Yes, Mister Wilde."

The lighting in the room was subdued but Jack caught the gleam in watery blue eyes, he had been put firmly in his place. Wilde continued the conversation; his voice was quiet but carried an authoritative timbre.

"I want you to work for me, Jack."

Wilkins' face registered surprise; Eric smiled.

"My firm deals in loans, protection, gambling and insurance. My operatives are well paid and I demand absolute loyalty."

"Where would I fit in?"

Wilde fixed Jack with a stare, eyes wide open.

"Everywhere, Jack, you will be free to pick up all the aspects of the business and if you have a particular forte – who knows, promotion is readily available."

"And my friends?"

"Your 'friends' Jack, will end up scrubbing prison floors particularly without your planning skills. Any more questions?"

"What happens if I say no?"

"You are free to walk away having missed a golden opportunity, but with the absolute certainty of fighting a losing battle with His Majesty's boys in blue."

Jack pondered the words, so eloquently delivered.

"When do I start?"

Eric Wilde stood up, he was taller than Jack had visualised. He offered his right hand, Jack stood up and took the handshake.

"Welcome, Jack," he nodded to one of his men who stepped to the desk and counted out a number of five pound notes. Jack looked at Wilde questioningly.

"It's an advance in pay, get yourself a decent suit, shirt and tie and let your shoes see some polish. Two things, Jack – no guns and we do not get involved in prostitution, is that clear?"

"Yes, Mister Wilde."

"Right, be here at nine o'clock tomorrow, you can walk home, it'll do you good!"

For the first time since his 'abduction' Jack smiled, I'm going to enjoy working for this man, he thought.

From day one in his new employment Jack Wilkins thrived. He delved into all the workings of the Wilde empire. He conversed with accountants, lawyers, customers and fellow employees, surprised at the size and complexity of the organisation. For two years he rarely saw the confines of the inner sanctum but, one day, Eric Wilde sent for him. Wilde was, as usual, behind his desk when Jack arrived, he smiled.

"Take a seat."

Jack looked around, nothing had changed, only one face was foreign to him, Eric followed his glance.

"May I introduce Terry Walker – he is to be my chief accountant."

The two men nodded, Walker was short, thin, his face pinched but his eyes constantly on the move as if he might miss something. A pair of pince-nez spectacles sat precariously on his nose. His grey hair was sparse, he was always happier when his bowler hat was in place. His dress was, for him, standard – dark suit, white shirt, black tie, burnished black shoes. For an instant Wilkins' mind went back to his schooldays and his reading – the spitting image of Dickens' Bob Crachit, he thought.

"Terry is going to show you the books, I want you to see into the heart of the set-up."

Jack was conscious of the glances which passed between the other occupants of the room.

Eric said, "Leave us, please."

Terry Walker guided Jack through the accounts. For two hours they studied columns of words and numbers all beautifully inscribed by Walker, Jack viewed the little man with a new-found respect. When the session ended Wilde moved a portrait of the King which was hanging on the wall behind him, the picture was hinged and it swung open to reveal a small safe. Wilde operated the combination lock, opened the door and placed the account books inside. He closed the safe, twirling the lock.

"Excuse us, Terry."

Walker gave a little bow and left the room. Wilde beckoned Jack to him. To his surprise Eric told him the combination to the safe and he practised the required operating manoeuvres, etching the numbers into his memory.

Eric Wilde was a master of deceit. He had built up his territory and sought the best cover for his illegal businesses. He began to subscribe to various charities and through these he came into contact with the Mayor of Birmingham, the local Chief Constable and allowed himself to come under public scrutiny. He attended all the functions to which he was invited and always requested three seats. Walker was introduced in his role as accountant and Wilkins as Wilde's chief executive. They became dubbed 'the three W's', Wilkins now acknowledged as being heir apparent to Wilde's empire. Once Jack suggested that Wilde expand his domain. Eric fielded the idea and turned.

"No, Jack, there is enough administration to do and any more to broaden our scope would no doubt create a violent reaction."

Jack fell silent. The status quo remained for another two years until Eric took Jack and Terry to a hotel in the country away from the sprawling city. They were accompanied by a chauffeur, there was little need for his services as the three W's relaxed together. It was Sunday evening when they headed home. They had settled down for the journey when the tractor trundled out of a field into their path. The police and ambulance men approached the vehicle at the same time. Fortunately there was no fire and access was relatively straightforward despite heavy damage to the car. The windscreen was smashed and both the chauffeur and Eric Wilde had frontal head injuries, the chauffeur would never drive again and Wilde was barely alive. Wilkins had been catapulted into the seat to his front. His face was covered in blood and more detailed examination revealed cuts, bruises and a broken right leg. Walker was the lucky one, only superficially damaged he was able to get to the ambulance unassisted. It fell to him to oversee the running of Wilde's business in his absence and he was relieved to see Jack come into the office albeit his leg was in plaster and he was on crutches. His facial injuries had healed quickly but a livid scar on his right cheek had changed his appearance, he now appeared to be quite fearsome. Unhesitatingly he made for Wilde's chair, Walker moved out of it accommodatingly.

Eric Wilde would not return. His recovery was slow, internal injuries had wreaked havoc and he would be on some type of painkilling medication for the rest of his life.

Jack Wilkins' reign began with some changes. The inner sanctum furniture, dark and antique, was replaced by a modern, lighter style. The office lighting was always full on; the new boss enjoyed plenty of illumination. Two new bodyguards appeared, both suited, both tough, but shorter than Wilkins – a nice touch, he thought. The introduction of a lissom, blonde young lady, Susan Latham, raised a few eyebrows. Ostensibly hired as a secretary it soon became apparent that her duties were not confined to the typewriter and filing cabinet. Wilkins maintained the ties with the local charities and dignitaries. They expressed sympathy with Wilde's condition, ignored Eric's scar and openly flirted with Susan, their wives tutting and noisily clearing their throats in the background.

Rumours of war began to seep into everyday lives. Eric 'Scarface' Wilkins pondered the ramifications of such an event. His empire would lose both employees and customers, he also considered the physical loss of property but put this to the back of his mind… for now! He also had to consider his own position with regard to active service – he had to show willing, certain people in society would expect it. Up until recently he had not deviated from Wilde's rules regarding guns and prostitution but some 'clients' had tested the resolve of the new regime. Wilkins quickly stamped out any intransigence, using a small task force of men with skills in arm-twisting. The Birmingham underworld was controlled by six 'bosses'. They all knew each other, two of them were militant and always at each other's throats. Phillip Reardon was an unknown quantity; his business was shrouded in mystery. He was rumoured to be a dealer in antiques, jewellery and painting. He was reputed to deal with lawyers, doctors, business executives, professional men who could afford to buy such items. Locally known as 'the quiet man', Reardon aroused Jack Wilkins' interest; this led to a private conversation with one of his men, Martin Edwards. He worked mainly in the gambling and protection arms of the set-up. Wilkins had noted the young man's obvious intelligence and had every confidence in his practical ability.

"Sit down, Martin."

Edwards looked around; Wilkins remembered his first visit to the office. Jack studied the face, long with pointed chin, clean-shaven, brown hair neat, inquisitive eyes, neatly dressed as in the old Wilde dictum.

"I have a job for you, Martin. There is a man in the city named Phillip Reardon. He is an accountant but also he deals, so it is said, in art treasures and his clients are well off. What I want you to do is infiltrate his business and report back to me, it may be useful to us to find out how he works… do you understand me?"

"Yes, Mister Wilkins, do you know where to find him?"

Jack passed him a piece of paper, Edwards read it, then slipped it into a pocket.

"Good luck."

Martin smiled "Thanks."

The next day, 3rd September 1939, war was declared. Months went by, the conflict seemed distant, detached. Millions of gas masks were issued; major cities saw their children evacuated to 'safer' areas. The general public saw trenches, anti-aircraft weapons and above these barrage balloons hovered. The necessity of these precautions were questioned but in April 1940 the European continent had undergone alarming radical change. The German military machine had invaded Norway, brushed the Netherlands and Belgium aside and the French were collapsing; the British Isles was under palpable threat. Jack Wilkins saw his staff dwindle as men were sucked into the Forces. He received one message only from Martin Edwards, it told him that Phillip Reardon was going to officers' training at Sandhurst, shortly after, Martin himself went into uniform. Wilkins filled his vacancies with older men and took steps to avoid his own involvement. He went through the motions and received a date for his medical. It was quite easy to find out who the duty doctor would be. He had a family, and a 'visit' by the Wilkins' heavy gang ensured that a serious 'respiratory' problem was discovered during the boss's examination.

The war proceeded, producing its heroes, disasters and victories. Despite the Blitz, Jack, Terry Walker and Susan were destined to survive. The office building remained unscathed by the bombing as did the organisation. Jack sent out feelers with regard to the black market which had arisen through rationing only to come, once more, into contact with the name 'Phillip Reardon'. It appeared that Reardon had cornered the petrol, food and clothing market very early in its inception. His administration was solid, the operatives he left to control things in his absence ran an extremely tight ship. Wilkins decided to leave well alone, his own profits were being maintained.

* * * * *

Martin Edwards walked into the office. Jack rose to meet him hand outstretched.

"You look well, Martin."

"You too, boss."

Edwards noted a few wrinkles, the hair was a little greyer but it added a more distinguished look, Wilkins was thinking that the war had taken its toll, Martin's face was lined, he looked older than he should.

"I'm working for Phillip Reardon."

Jack's interest soared.

"A mate and I take a barge loaded with black market goods to Worcester."

Wilkins looked keenly at Martin.

"Reardon wants to sell his business."

"How much of it?"

"All of it."

"Why, Martin?"

"He and his family are moving to France."

Jack paced up and down the office, his hands clasped behind him, thinking. Finally he made his way back to his desk.

"I reckon we should get down to brass tacks, Martin, tell me all you know about Mister Reardon."

Valerie opened the door to find herself facing three men. The one immediately to her front bore a scar, one was small, thin, the third was obviously a bodyguard, he was well dressed and carried a permanent scowl – built like a tank, thought Valerie. Wilkins spoke, "I'm Jack, this is Terry and Arthur."

"Please come in, gentlemen, you are expected."

She led them into the drawing room where they found Phillip Reardon. So this is the great man, thought Wilkins as he smiled and moved forward to meet the host. The door to the room was firmly closed and business began. Due to their both being accountants, Phillip and Terry soon established a friendly rapport and they carried out most of the discussion which disconcerted Jack a little. The wheeling and dealing took well over an hour to resolve but agreement was reached and Reardon poured drinks, Wilkins and Walker appreciated the quality of the liquor.

"Did you actually buy this, Phillip, or did it fall off the back of a lorry?"

Reardon smiled "Gentlemen, a toast… to a good, honest, profit."

They touched glasses, smiling at the 'honest' bit. The three men left the house on the hill, Terry's briefcase was heavy with account books.

"Well, Terry, how did we do?"

"Very fair, Jack, very fair."

* * * * *

Maria Rinaldi crashed to the floor, a cut at the corner of her mouth bleeding. Gino raised his foot to kick his wife but she rolled up into a protective ball.

"Bitch!"

Maria's cheeks glistened with tears, she looked up at Gino.

"Why Maria, Guilio Belucchi is an old, illiterate peasant?"

Maria sobbed, "He was kind to me and you were never here, always in your beloved hospital."

"So it's my fault?"

"Partly but you don't have all the story… I'm pregnant!"

Gino was shouting now, "I suppose it's his?"

"I don't know."

"So… it could be mine?"

"Yes," Maria got to her feet.

"And when can we expect this child to appear?"

"Six months from now."

He moved toward her, she recoiled.

"How did you find out?"

"A private detective, certain things gave you away, more often than not in our bed!"

Maria looked into Gino's eyes.

"What happens now?"

"The Rinaldi name will not be dragged through the mire, we cannot afford any scandal… and Belucchi will cease to be part of your life, is that agreed… Maria?"

"Yes," she said, quietly.

Gino strode from the room.

Guilio Belucchi's daughter Claudia yawned as she walked into the kitchen. Guilio smiled, "Have you seen your brother this morning?"

"No he's still in bed, maybe."

"He's normally all ready to go at this time of day."

"Shall I take a look, Father?"

"Yes."

Claudia soon returned.

"His bed hasn't been slept in, he must have found a girl somewhere."

Guilio looked at Sophia, they were both unconvinced. Their feelings turned to misgivings as the day wore on. Guilio could not settle and he and Claudia left their employees to their own devices. They searched the local village as well as they could and, having drawn a blank, they reported to the one available policeman. He was sympathetic and said he would do what he could but failed to leave Guilio or Claudia very encouraged. They returned home hoping to find Enrico but they only found Sophia, alone and despondent. Days went by, the days went into weeks, the weeks into months, Enrico did not return. On a whim Guilio carried out a search of the Rinaldi castle but it revealed no clues. Sophia's health went into decline, Guilio's normal vitality waned, he aged quickly spending a lot of time sat somewhere brooding. Claudia did her best to instil some life into the Villa Belucchi but it was a hopeless task. Her mother died, people said she died of a broken heart. Guilio descended into deeper gloom, Claudia took it upon herself to look after her father's every need. Every day she looked down the track which led to the house but the vision she sought never materialised.

Claudia frowned, a car had pulled up at the front door. She went into the yard wiping her hands on her pinafore as she went. A man walked towards her, he was quite tall and wore a charcoal grey suit. As he drew nearer his features bore a certain familiarity, Claudia guessed his age as being in the early thirties.

"Hello... I'm Frederico Rinaldi."

Claudia was nonplussed, but only for a moment.

"Can I help you?"

"I have come to discuss business with you."

Claudia hesitated... "You had better come inside."

They moved indoors, Guilio heard their entrance and looked up.

"We have a visitor, Father – Frederico Rinaldi."

For an instant fire burned in Guilio's eyes, but the flames soon flickered and died, his energy spent. Claudia took Frederico's arm and directed him to another room beckoning him to a chair.

"I will come straight to the point, Miss Belucchi, we wish to buy your vineyard."

Claudia was dumbfounded. Frederico continued, his voice quiet but firm.

"It would appear that you could be in trouble. Your father is unable to function as he once did, this leaves you alone to deal with the land and care for him at the same time."

Claudia was angry. "You think I can't do this, what gives you the right to come here and poke around in our personal lives?"

Frederico raised a hand, anticipating a torrent of words.

"Listen... Claudia, we buy the property and take a reasonable profit, you choose an overseer in the fields, you retain all your employees and secure your own future at the same time, how does that sound?"

"And what guarantee can you give me that all this will happen?"

"A proper contract signed in the presence of lawyers."

"Why this sudden concern for the Belucchi family?"

"Not so many years ago your father saved my parents' lives, it has not been forgotten; although I admit our interest is predominately business."

"I need time to think but there will be one condition, my father must never know of this arrangement."

"Agreed," Frederico gave her a card.

"When you have decided call me."

Claudia nodded and showed Frederico out of the villa by a side door. She heard the car move away, she looked at Guilio, he seemed not to notice.

Claudia took stock of her circumstances. The villa itself and the outhouses needed repair. The once beautiful gardens were totally neglected, everything was overgrown and the stream failed to flow properly. Claudia came to the only decision possible. She spoke confidentially to her Aunt Lina, and contracts were exchanged at her house. Claudia offered the post of overseer to a man who knew the wine business well and would command the respect of the workers. His promotion was accompanied by a celebration at which Guilio nodded and laughed with his companions, Claudia was content. The necessary repairs took place, the vines yielded a good harvest and the Belucchi employees were given some time off.

It was warm already; the sun was barely in the sky as Claudia prepared breakfast for her and Guilio. A babble of noise caused her to go to the window. All the vineyard workers were there, most of them carrying tools, Claudia opened the front door. The overseer touched his cap.

"What's going on?"

"We are going to restore the gardens, get the place as it was."

"That's very kind of you."

"You look after us well, Miss, now it's our turn to really do something for you and the Master," he moved away.

Claudia closed the door, tears not far away. For two days the Belucchi staff toiled in the sun, a saw could be heard cutting wood, soil was weeded, plants, trees and hedges tended and the stream once again flowed between mown lawns. A brand new seat replaced Guilio's old one, his pleasure at this gift created some deep emotion. Claudia gazed in wonder at the results of her employee's labour. She could only show her gratitude in one way… it was time for yet another celebration, this time at the Villa Belucchi!

* * * * *

Constable Ray Hopper had changed noticeably over recent years. He had lost weight and with it his joviality and vitality. His long-suffering wife Sally patiently supported him and did her utmost to keep the children Geoff and Molly happy. When they were alone Ray and Sally discussed the hold David Collins had on them. They had to admit that the bribes had provided a better life for them… but at what cost?

It was a night the same as any other. "I'm going to take a good look at the 'patch', Sally, don't wait up."

She looked at him, there was a change in his demeanour, his eyes, usually dull these days, displayed a new light, his shoulders weren't hunched. Sally knew that her husband had come to a decision, she said nothing.

Joe Thompson, Martin Edwards and John Mooney transferred the load from the barge to the van. Little conversation took place and Edwards never talked about his boss and 'Scarface' Wilkins deemed it unnecessary to interfere whatsoever with the Worcester element of his empire. The van loaded, Joe drove away, a watcher in the darkness moved out of cover and made his way home.

Inspector Frank Morris stood looking out of his office window. Behind him Ray Hopper was writing a statement, it was lengthy and precise. Morris went to the door and asked a member of staff for two cups of tea and then he settled down to study the policeman's words. The regular ticking of a clock was the only sound in the room, being disturbed only when Morris moved the pages of the document. At last he was finished and faced Hopper.

"Well, Constable Hopper, a fine kettle of fish!" Ray remained silent.

"Do you know when the next shipment is?"

"No, sir."

"This means tying men to the canal night after night."

"Afraid so, sir."

"Right, Constable Hopper, return to your duties I want everything to appear normal, understood?"

He stood up and went to the door and was almost through it when Morris spoke again.

"Ray!"

Hopper turned, "Sir?"

"You've done the right thing."

Five nights later Edwards, Mooney and Thompson were arrested along with the contraband and the keys to Collins' yard.

David Collins was enjoying a leisurely breakfast when the heavy knock of the law came on his door, Vera Lewis fainted when George was taken into custody later that morning. Although overcome by events herself Grace Thompson came to revive and comfort Vera, they were destined to support each other manfully through the difficult times ahead. Des Hilton's flat was raided, no response came to their knock so the police summoned the landlord. A speedy search revealed that the place was empty and all signs suggested that it had been that way for some time.

Inspector Frank Morris, accompanied by a sergeant, interviewed George Lewis, whose solicitor was present. George looked frail and tired but answered all Morris's questions. He admitted starting the black market business in St Paul's and the recruitment of Joe Thompson although he attempted to exonerate him by relating to his situation regarding marriage to Margaret Collins.

"Who were your customers, George?"

"Various people, all over the place."

"You kept books?"

"Yes."

"Where are they now, George?"

"David Collins had them."

"How did Collins find out about the business?"

"Through Joe, he is Collins' brother-in-law and there were questions about Joe's working hours... one thing led to another."

"Did Collins know about your arrangement with Ray Hopper?"

"Yes, he knew everything, he threatened to expose me to the police if I did not sell the business to him."

"When did he buy the business, George?"

"November 1944."

"That's it for now, gentlemen, make sure George has a cup of tea," Morris said.

David Collins was smartly dressed, as was his representative of the law. Morris took some moments to size up the alleged offender, mentally noting the hate in the eyes. From the beginning of the interview it was clear that Collins had no defence but appeared to derive great pleasure when naming Phillip Reardon, Desmond Hilton and the Simmonds brothers as his accomplices.

"What about Edwards and Mooney?" asked Morris.

"Hired by Reardon, they only made a few runs, I never met them."

Maureen Collins shuddered inwardly as the footfalls of policemen echoed around the house; young Brian Thompson's eyes followed the sounds as if he could sense that all was not well. The law had arrived early with a search warrant, they had been in the house for nearly two hours and there were bags in the hall waiting to be removed. Maureen was deep in thought and failed to hear a young police officer approaching.

"We're finished, ma'am."

Maureen came out of her reverie, startled.

"Oh... right!"

The front door slammed, an eerie silence settled on the house. Maureen looked at her grandson, she picked him up.

"Let's go eat, young man."

Harold and Margaret had decided to open the shop as usual; Maureen wished they were here now.

Frank Morris spoke to his counterparts in the Birmingham police force. Based on the statement given by David Collins a group of police officers moved in on the house on the hill in Northfield; it was completely empty, not one item left to identify the previous occupants. The investigation continued, Jim and Jean Simmonds were visited, they told the police that their sons were working somewhere in Europe and had been for some time, Jim confirmed that contact was rare. Phillip Reardon came under the microscope and enquiries led to a liaison between the police and the Ministry of Defence. Edwards and Mooney were found to have no criminal records but they both maintained that they had acquired the job on the barge during a conversation with a stranger in their 'local'. Questioned separately their description of the stranger tallied and both said that the barge was already loaded before they set sail for Worcester. Frank Morris began to sift through the information that was available and decided that the case could turn out to be a lengthy, complicated business... how right he was!

Terry Walker came into the office, one glance at Jack Wilkins' face was enough.

"Trouble, Jack?"

"The barge hasn't come back from Worcester... maybe it's sunk," he said sarcastically.

"I know an accountant in Worcester, I'll call him," Walker reached for a telephone. The conversation was surprisingly short. Wilkins looked up, "Well?"

"The whole Worcester crowd have been nabbed, it's all over the local rag."

"Great!" Jack muttered, then a thought occurred to him.

"Edwards... he could sell us down the river, Terry."

"Not a chance, he's much too fly for that. He's ambitious Jack, besides, the coppers would have been here by now."

"I wish I had your confidence."

"Rest easy, I will square up the books, the Worcester set-up never existed."

"Thanks, Terry, what would I do without you?"

"Sink like the barge."

They both chuckled.

The headlines read, 'Wheelchair Rogue Arrested'. The main body of the report began, 'Former Army Lieutenant David Collins of St Paul's, Worcester, was arrested today...' A tear fell onto the print, Maureen let the newspaper slip to the floor. Harold put his arm round his wife's shoulder in an attempt to console her. A sad-faced Margaret sat across the room from them.

"There is something else."

Harold and Maureen stared at their daughter.

"I'm pregnant again."

Maureen buried her head in her hands. Silence prevailed for some minutes, the clock in the room ticked on remorselessly as it did in Frank Morris's office. It was Harold who ended the prolonged agony.

"We can safely assume that David and Joe will go to prison."

He waited patiently for the resultant sobbing to subside.

"David's room will be empty, Margaret's room is available, she and the children can move back in."

"And the house?" asked Margaret.

"We rent it out, then when Joe comes back…"

"Every cloud has a silver lining," murmured Maureen.

The defendants were arraigned in court the following day, all were released on bail, emotional reunions took place at the Collins' and Lewis' households, although Harold displayed a great deal of reticence towards his only son, Maureen noticed but left the situation to resolve itself… hopefully.

A big, black, shiny car swept into the yard at the side of Worcester Police Station. From the rear seat came the local Chief Constable and a younger man in a pinstriped suit, he carried a bowler hat and a furled umbrella. They moved quickly through a side door and made their way to Frank Morris's office where he was waiting with his Superintendent. Introductions took place, the young man was from the Foreign Office. One hour later the big car left Worcester heading for a police station in Birmingham. Frank Morris sat deep in thought for some moments before reaching for his telephone. He spoke at length to two solicitors. Tea had arrived during the Home Office visit, it had been left and gone cold… he went to the door and ordered another!

St Paul's was dismal, the rain poured from the skies. Drains filled to overflowing, roads turned to rivers and water streamed from broken guttering. Very few people attempted to penetrate the deluge but some had little choice. Two taxis splashed their way to the Collins' and Lewis' homes. The passengers piled in quickly and many a curtain twitched as the cars pulled away, their destination Worcester Crown

Court. Prior to his appearance in court, David Collins' solicitor spoke with him primarily to discuss procedure.

"I suppose Reardon, Hilton and the Simmonds are in court in Birmingham today?"

"No."

Collins looked puzzled.

"When... then?"

"They are not appearing at all."

"What?"

"Insufficient evidence."

David's laugh was sardonic.

"You are joking... right?"

"Only Worcester people are involved in this case."

Collins' frown was deep, thoughtful.

"So George, Joe and I are carrying the can for everyone?"

"You could put it like that, yes."

David exploded, furious. Wisely the solicitor remained quiet until the verbal storm passed.

"You must exercise restraint in court, Mister Collins, it could make matters worse."

Collins stared at the man for a moment then lapsed into a brooding silence.

The three defendants were gathered in the dock. Lewis and Thompson stood forlorn, Collins glared about him from his wheelchair. Faced by a guilty plea from all parties the judge listened to representations from the relevant solicitors before passing sentence. The members of family, one or two interested onlookers and two policemen, including Frank Morris listened intently as the punishments were meted out. George Lewis was described as an opportunist, going against his past business record. He was given a four-year suspended sentence. The judge told him that his age had saved him from prison. Grace Thompson steadied Vera as she slumped forward in anguish, then listened stoically as her son was said to be misguided and sent to gaol for three years, Margaret wept openly. There was a momentary pause before the judge continued, then...

"David Collins you have pleaded guilty to all the charges brought against you. The investigation into this case has revealed you to be embittered and ruthless. You have used blackmail and guile to achieve your goals, both you and George Lewis fought for your country but you have emerged as tarnished heroes. You will go to prison for seven years, take him down!"

There was a stunned silence as Collins turned to leave the dock, for an instant his eyes met those of his father – Harold had seen that look before. He said nothing and led the families out of the court, there would be time for an inquest later.

Frank Morris went back to his office, for a moment he leafed through the file on his desk before placing it in the relevant cabinet. He went to his office door and opened it to be faced by a smiling young officer.

"Thought you might like this, sir."

"Thank you," Frank winked as he took the mug of tea. Later both he and Jack Wilkins received the news that Martin Edwards and John Mooney had been fined and released, a satisfactory result for all concerned.

It was with a heavy heart that Constable Ray Hopper tendered his resignation from the police force. Certain factions of the profession wanted to bring criminal charges against him but the good name of the force had entered the discussion regarding his future, this point prevailed. Frank Morris interviewed him and one week later Ray, Sally and the children left Worcester with their furniture. Morris had contacted a colleague in London, told him the facts surrounding the Hopper case and the family moved into a rented flat and Ray became a night watchman in a factory, grateful for the chance to redeem himself.

Marilyn Cooper went to the local police station and reported the missing Paul Parker. A thorough investigation took place but the trail ran cold in Berlin. Two policemen visited Peter and Elizabeth Parker. Their enquiries were met by an indifference that surprised them.

"They didn't show much concern did they?" said one.

"I'm sorry we disturbed them," his companion shrugged.

None of them would guess that the missing man's body would become a tiny part of the German capital's new infrastructure or that a large amount of money lay in a Swiss bank account waiting to be claimed.

* * * * *

Phillip Reardon and André Dupont had enjoyed coffee before moving to their respective desks. Important documents lay ready for perusal but neither man had made much headway before the telephone rang. André took the call, it lasted some minutes before he replaced the receiver, he looked across at Phillip.

"That was a friend from your Foreign Office. We need to protect our team, it would be unwise for them to return to England. Your position was always safe but Des, Mike and Tony are now vulnerable following certain events, the organisation they were part of had an unforeseen weak link."

"Hilton can be very useful to us, with him speaking French and German he can be employed here. I would suggest that Mike and Tony revert to the building trade – half of Europe needs rebuilding."

"Sounds practical."

"I will call them in and we can sort out details, although I believe Des has formed a romantic relationship in Berlin."

"Yes, André, very much like someone I know not a million miles away!"

Dupont smiled, "To work, Reardon, lots to do."

Phillip saluted, "Yes, sir!"

He marched to his desk and sat down, both men laughed, comfortable together.

André and Phillip soon found themselves deeply involved in the planning of Europe's recovery from the war. Many discussions took place following an offer of aid by the United States which came to be known as the Marshall Plan. Delegates from Britain, France and other European countries met in Paris and a rebuilding programme set in motion. Initially sixteen countries agreed to cooperate and administer the project; André Dupont's dream was taking shape.

Slowly Berlin began to live again. Des and Frieda found places to eat and indulged in musical evenings as instruments which had lain idle for long periods came back into use. Their relationship flourished and one evening after having dinner in a small restaurant, Des proposed. He had managed to find a jeweller and have a ring made for the occasion. Frieda's eyes lit up as she accepted both Des and the ring; later they strolled arm in arm through the city, their thoughts on the future, their eyes only for each other.

The following day Des and the Simmonds brothers were summoned to Paris. Frieda was tearful but put on a brave face when Hilton gave her the news.

"Don't worry, Frieda, I'll be back before you know it."

"I hope so."

Des slipped an arm round her shoulders.

"I'm holding my future at the moment, I won't be letting it go, that's for sure."

She looked up into his face, "Hurry back, darling."

"I will."

Three days later Hilton returned.

"We have been offered a job."

"We?"

"Yes, Frieda, we would be employed to help rebuild Europe and then unify it under one banner."

"Sounds a noble idea, who runs the operation?"

"André Dupont, a friend of my business associate, Phillip Reardon."

"When would we start?"

"We have time to put our personal affairs in order, if we take the job on."

"Can we go and see this Dupont, Des?"

"It can be arranged."

Frieda shrugged, kissed him, "Arrange it, my love."

André, Celine, Des, Frieda, Phillip and Valerie were sat in a Paris restaurant overlooking the river Seine. The atmosphere and scenery created the perfect setting for dinner and relaxed conversation. André spoke of his passion for Europe, mainly for the benefit of Des and Frieda, and then he sat back as the ladies talked among themselves. The evening came to its inevitable end.

Two days later Des Hilton contacted André. Dupont put the telephone down and looked at Phillip. Phillip looked up, "What?"

"That was Des Hilton… we have a team!"

"Good!"

"That's not all, Phillip."

"Go on."

"The night of the party Celine and I… decided to get married!"

Phillip came round his desk. Joyfully he clasped his old friend's hand.

"This is great news, André, congratulations."

"Thank you, I think this calls for another party."

"Leave it to me, my dear fellow."

Once again the group met for dinner and the celebration of André and Celine's proposed wedding. They were all enjoying after-dinner drinks when Phillip spoke.

"Why don't we have a double wedding?"

There was a pause as the words sank in. Someone said "Why not?"

The party descended into a babble as the idea caught fire. Des and Frieda looked at each other.

"Well?"

"As someone said, why not?"

One month later the double wedding took place in a small church on the Left Bank of the Seine. The Simmonds brothers, Mike and Tony, acted as best men and a small number of guests witnessed the ceremony. The reception was held in a beautiful garden close to the church, the sun shone and everyone enjoyed the excellent cuisine. A quartet provided music and people attracted by the sound came to watch and smile at the proceedings before moving away. It was during the dancing that a motorcycle messenger came to find André. He took the envelope and frowned as he opened it. His expression changed dramatically as he read it, it was a personal note of congratulation from Charles de Gaulle! Des Hilton stood aside from the crowd to enjoy a drink, Frieda came to him.

"And how is my 'rubble woman'?"

"Your 'rubble woman' is fine."

"André has given us two whole days off."

"That's big of him," said Frieda as she held on to the arm of her new husband. Des Hilton looked down at her, for a fleeting moment he thought about David Collins, Florence and the wheelchair… but it was only a fleeting moment!

* * * * *

A letter from Frederico Rinaldi informed Claudia Belucchi that a contract had been signed by one, Umberto Rossi, to provide bottles for the wine. Production at the vineyard was high and the present system needed change; cost had been a strong factor influencing the decision. Claudia locked the letter away in a desk drawer, she had set up a small office and much to her relief her father rarely entered the room. Andrea Rossi, son of Umberto, personally formed part of the delivery team, he also produced the distribution list. The Rossi organisation was new to the area but were determined to make an impact. Andrea met Claudia on his rounds, his first impressions were that she was nothing special. At first their conversations were sparse but Umberto encouraged Andrea to devote more time to talking to the customers, it was good for relations and business. Andrea obeyed and was surprised by Claudia's business acumen. He mentioned this fact to Umberto.

"Listen to the young lady, Andrea, use her knowledge to widen your own. She knows her employees, she is part of them, they are part of her. Take a close look at the Villa Belucchi and its gardens, they are maintained by her workers in their spare time. This is a result of years of genuine love and respect between employer and employee, a model for us all."

"Yes, Father."

From then on Andrea saw Claudia in a different light. She had considered Andrea cold at their initial meetings but his new approach impressed her. She gave him the opportunity to visit the Villa Belucchi and he accepted. He met Guilio and the pair strolled through the gardens.

"Your father, is he well?"

"Yes... why?"

"He seemed a little distant."

"Some months ago my brother Enrico disappeared and Father has never recovered from it."

"I see, any clues?"

"Nothing."

Andrea fell silent, mulling over the situation.

"I'm sorry, Claudia."

She smiled, reached out and touched his arm.

"Thank you for your concern."

"May I see you again, Claudia? I've enjoyed our walk."

"Yes," she said, without hesitation.

Slowly a bond of companionship and trust grew between the couple. They openly talked about their lives and families. Claudia spoke of the Rinaldi affair and they went to the castle ruins. Mother nature was gradually covering the building with vegetation but there were paths where people still wandered through.

"Where are the Rinaldis now?"

"In Florence."

"You don't see them any more?"

"No," Claudia said, she felt it prudent not to discuss the ownership of the vineyard just yet.

Claudia was darning a pair of Guilio's socks, they were worn out really but he insisted that they could be repaired. He was dozing in his favourite chair and Claudia started a little when he spoke.

"I like the young man that brings the bottles, Andrea isn't it?"

She was pleasantly surprised, "You do, Father?"

"Yes, he seems a friendly, cheerful man, maybe you should go out with him more often."

"Yes, Father," Claudia beamed.

Umberto accompanied his son on his bottle delivery; they both knew it was a deliberate ploy to meet Claudia. Andrea introduced them. He likened them to two fencers as Umberto asked questions which Claudia answered and then came back with enquiries of her own. Occasionally she glanced at Andrea and smiled and he realised that she was relishing the conversation with his father. At their departure Umberto graciously kissed Claudia's hand.

"I sincerely hope that we will meet again, my dear, and in the very near future."

Claudia blushed and gave a little curtsy.

"Thank you, sir," she said, eyes twinkling.

When they were alone Umberto turned to his son.

"What a pleasant young lady and with brains too. She would make quite a catch, Andrea, handle her with care."

"Yes, Father."

Three months later Andrea and Claudia announced their engagement, much to the delight of everyone concerned. After only another three months they became husband and wife. The wedding took place in the local church and once again the old village square rang to the sound of music, dancing and the hubbub of joviality. The couple would live at the Villa Belucchi with Guilio, and Claudia noted with pleasure that on this day he looked much like his old self. The arrival of two grandchildren partly erased the loss of his wife and son and he began to show interest in the vineyard again but he would never know Claudia's secret. She had told Andrea of her business dealings with Frederico Rinaldi and he had accepted the situation.

Marcello Rinaldi was thriving. He had handed the reins of business to Frederico and entered the political arena. He had learned many things from his period with the Fascist regime. It had served to portray the real feelings of the people and he had used this knowledge to great advantage. Coupling this with his financial clout he rapidly made inroads into his new world. The established politicians in the area listened to his ideas on reform and the majority were impressed and he was quickly accepted into their circle. He was handed the task of evaluating projects in the region and allocating the necessary monies to complete the venture, with hierarchy approval. Marcello had always had power but never such as this and he became intoxicated by it but, fortunately for him, his wife Natalia was always there as a steadying influence.

Gino Rinaldi had watched his father adopt the mantle of politician with interest. He, himself, had power of his own even over life and death. He reasoned that power came at a price and, with that in mind, he made a great effort to resolve his marital problems with Maria. She bore a son, they called him Luigi, after Gino's ancestor. He looked like Maria but when he grew older he would display mannerisms foreign to the Rinaldi family, this made even Marcello think but where he thrust the notion away Gino and Maria knew that the child was Guilio Belucchi's. Eighteen months after his arrival in the world Luigi had a brother, Giovanni. The baby was received with great joy and cemented the marriage which had almost foundered, there was much to look forward to. Everything appeared to be running smoothly for the Rinaldi family, their destiny to control seemingly intact, but any complacency could prove dangerous...

Part Eight

RESURRECTION AND RETRIBUTION

ITALY, LATE 1945

Located at the edge of the village square the local bar was, as usual, busy. Not too large, the place had a character all of its own. It had provided a meeting place for the community for five decades. The bar ran the full length of the rear wall, shelves displayed products for sale. Ageing wooden tables and chairs creaked ominously under the weight of drinks and customers. The bar floor was wooden, scarred by years of use; it received a daily sweep which raised clouds of dust that quickly settled down again. The walls and ceiling had seen two licks of paint in their lifetime, cobwebs gathered in corners undisturbed and smoke from candles and pipes had discoloured exposed surfaces. The bar was owned by the Barone family. Guiseppe and his daughter Carla spent most of their lives in the building. Guiseppe was of average height, his head bald apart from a scattering of hair around his ears. As if to counteract this he sported a large moustache, only clipped when Carla reminded him. He was portly and usually appeared before his clientele wearing a shirt with sleeves rolled up, grey trousers and once-black shoes cracked and dust-covered. Round his middle he wore an apron, its cleanliness, thankfully, controlled by Carla. His brown eyes were lively and bright. His voice was loud but his sense of humour attracted both local customers and the rare stranger into conversation with him, he was the ultimate inn-keeper. Carla, married with one daughter, was Guiseppe's best friend. She helped out in every aspect of the bar including manhandling barrels in the cellar. Amply proportioned she tended to wear low-cut dresses, her bodily curves attracting male eyes like magnets, rumour had it that her assets accounted for half the company being there!

Enjoying the warm, friendly atmosphere was Enrico Belucchi. A number of men in the bar worked in his father's vineyard and he was playing cards with three of them. Enrico had looked up and smiled at Carla a couple of times, she had reciprocated. She had had designs on him once but he had shown little interest and she had drifted into other relationships. Enrico glanced at his watch, it was time to go. He excused himself from the card game, bade his companions farewell and stepped out into the street. Darkness enveloped him, few lights were showing. Soon he was approaching the edge of the village, about to pass the last house before joining the track that led to his home. For the moment he paused, the sky revealed few stars and there was a hint of rain in the night air, his thoughts turned to the vineyard. A sound behind him made him turn, he hardly felt the expertly delivered blow that rendered him unconscious and he knew nothing of the two men hoisting him unceremoniously into a waiting car which was immediately set in motion, heading out into the countryside. There had been no witnesses to the attack.

Enrico came to, whatever he was lying on was cold and his body bounced, he picked up the noise of an engine. Someone spoke and he felt a sharp pain in the arm, he descended back into the world of darkness. Later he woke. This time he was lying on something soft and movement was up and down, again there was an engine, a quieter, throbbing sound. Unconsciousness closed in on him once more. The next time he awoke he found himself being jolted on a hard surface, he was sweating. Again he heard an engine, it intermittently roared and whined. He heard voices loud and harsh. His descent into oblivion this time was a blessing.

The light coming through the windows dazzled Enrico for some moments as his eyes tried to focus. Soon he could make out a white ceiling and a slowly turning fan. Gingerly he turned his head from side to side, he felt no pain. He was in a bed, the sheets were crisp and he lifted the top one. His one item of clothing was a loin cloth, there were bruises on various parts of his body. He lowered the sheet and sat up to take stock of his surroundings. He was in a big room, his eyes were drawn to a series of arches. Some formed parts of windows, others were filled with wooden latticework screens, some housed items of furniture and one contained the room's door. The architecture was foreign to Enrico, it was certainly not Italian. He was allowed no more time for thought as the door opened and a figure entered. The man was slight of build, his dark features topped by a mixture of black and grey hair cropped short. He had a neatly trimmed beard, an aquiline nose and dark, hooded eyes. His dress was a long grey robe, his feet bore sandals. Despite his stature Enrico noted the measured walk, the shoulders back, the body perfectly upright; this was a man of authority. He approached the bed.

"Do you speak English?"

The voice level, concise, clear.

"Yes, I can get by."

There was a slight trace of a smile.

"That is good, welcome to the house of Sheikh El-Quasimi."

Enrico frowned, collected himself.

"May I ask where I am?"

"You may, you are in the Sahara desert in the country of Algeria."

Enrico looked at the man, aghast.

"Can I ask how and why I have been brought here?"

"No."

"Can I ask who is responsible for my… kidnapping?"

"No."

The finality and weight of authority in the answers deterred Enrico from pursuing the matter any further. The robed man, in complete command of the conversation, paused and sensed the young man coming to terms with his situation. At length he gauged that the inner turmoil had quietened a little, he bowed.

"I am Mahmoud, Lieutenant to El-Quasimi."

"I am Enrico Belucchi."

"Yes, may I call you Rico?"

"Lots of people do."

"Good, then Rico it shall be, how do you feel?"

"I feel well."

"That too is good, it is true that a young body can overcome adversity very quickly. There are bathing facilities through that arch, you will find the water cold but refreshing, I shall return with food and clothing."

Mahmoud gave a little bow and strode from the room. Later the door opened and a boy entered, followed by Mahmoud. The youngster was barefoot, wore a white robe with a red sash about the waist and a fez. He carried a tray of food and a small cup. The boy went to a table, his eyes studying Enrico. Mahmoud uttered some word and the boy, startled, almost spilled the contents of the cup. He left the room quickly, head down.

"You must forgive him, he has seen few foreigners close up."

Enrico shrugged, looked at the food.

"Pasta?"

"Very similar to your Italian dish but we call it couscous. It is our main diet and comes with most meals including sweet dishes. The meat you have is chicken and there are dates. The drink is coffee, you will find it bitter, it is an acquired taste."

Mahmoud watched with satisfaction as Enrico ate, he was hesitant with the coffee but he was thirsty and emptied the cup. Mahmoud clapped his hands once and the boy came in. He moved much more quickly this time, Enrico received only a cursory glance.

Enrico looked up, "Will I die here, Mahmoud?"

"Only Allah knows that, Rico."

"Or the sheikh."

Mahmoud chose to ignore the latter remark and clapped his hands again.

The boy carried two robes, Mahmoud held one out to Enrico who slipped it over his head.

"How do I look?"

Mahmoud took in the grey robe and Enrico's looks.

"Your skin is already burned by the sun, your appearance among our people will hardly be noticed, come I will show you your new home, there are sandals by the door."

Mahmoud led Enrico out of the room and through a labyrinth of corridors and spacious halls. He found himself faced by opulence beyond his wildest dreams. The ceilings were high, white, the walls painted in pastel shades. The floor was marble interspersed with colourful mosaic. There were more latticework screens, few rugs, but furniture of obvious high quality. Presently they approached a door which was flanked by two armed guards.

"That is the sheikh's private quarters," Mahmoud said.

"Will I ever meet him?"

"Maybe tomorrow, one month, one year, who knows?"

Enrico fell silent, continuing to drink in the surrounding riches. Eventually Mahmoud led him down some steps and out into a courtyard. Out here the heat was oppressive and Enrico felt sweat form under his robe. He caught his breath for a few moments, Mahmoud was aware of his predicament.

"You will soon get used to the climate; the temperature will drop this evening, it freezes in the winter months."

Mahmoud set a brisk pace, there was much ground to cover. It soon became obvious to Enrico that he was in a fortress. It was square, made of stone, the walls high above him, round towers at each corner. He noted that the ramparts were liberally manned by sentries, his thoughts returned to the guards at the sheikh's quarters. There were just two structures in the area, an open-top water tank and a low single-storied building, it had no windows and was secured by a steel door. Entrance to the fort was provided by a main gate, its massive wooden doors open now, a postern gate was in another wall and this was where Mahmoud headed. They came out into what was the local oasis. There was a small, cloudy pool, two tents and a few palm trees. Three waist-high walls were strategically placed in front of the postern, put there as a temporary defensive measure, mused Enrico. Nearby was a small mosque, its stone walls had seen better days, its roof, discoloured by years of changing weather, had once been a masterpiece of craftsmanship. This building, as Enrico was soon to realise, was an integral part of the community and not to be neglected. Testimony to this was borne out by the rude scaffolding and loin-clothed masons at work. A minaret looked practically new, someone was at its apex even as Enrico watched. There was a football pitch, rough poles were nailed together to form the goals. Mahmoud glanced at his companion.

"Do you play, Rico?"

"No we were far too busy."

"When it is cooler many will play, you will be asked to join in, you can be sure."

Enrico smiled. The pair wandered into a camp comprised of a number of large black tents. Here were men, women and animals. Various smells assailed the nostrils, Enrico sneezed, someone laughed. At their approach work stopped, some men stood at attention, the master's lieutenant was among them. Mahmoud stopped and waved Enrico into one of the tents. A man stood up to greet them. He was taller than Mahmoud, and wider. To Enrico's surprise the men embraced each other before a hand was stretched out to him, he was shaking hands with his future teacher, Ahmed.

Mahmoud spoke, "Ahmed will teach you our language, how to ride, shoot and how to survive in the desert. Make good use of his talents, they may save your life one day."

Ahmed's voice was deep but not unfriendly.

"Come, sit, we will take tea together, tomorrow your teaching begins."

Enrico was introduced to mint tea and while he sipped it he studied Ahmed. He had a large face, most of it covered by hair. A small round cap sat on his head but it was almost lost among his black curls. He had a full beard, there were a few grey hairs to be found here. He had a big, patrician's nose but his eyes portrayed his character – almost as black as his hair they caught all available light and danced and smiled, enhanced by prominent crow's feet. When he moved he moved with the stealth of a lion, the hunter! He was not fat, he was muscular, very much like his own father, Enrico thought.

Mahmoud and Enrico dined together, this time it was couscous, lamb and vegetables, the chef had added herbs and spices and Enrico drank lots of water. Mahmoud smiled. Left alone Enrico took time to reflect on his position. He had literally been torn from one lifestyle and dropped into another. He thought about his father, Guilio, his mother, Sophia, his sister Claudia, his friends and the vineyard – Italy was his homeland, that's where he should be. There was no proof but he guessed that the Rinaldis were responsible for his kidnap, but why? That afternoon he had looked at the Sahara, the sand dunes, the sky. He had noticed a track, a man and a donkey had come along it as he watched – I must find out where it goes, he thought. Ahmed taught Enrico almost nothing in the next few days, neither did he attempt to.

"Rico's mind is elsewhere, he is certainly not with us."

Mahmoud touched his arm, "Be ready, you will be needed very soon."

Ahmed nodded, his face unusually grave.

It was midnight, cool but light with a beautiful clear sky and a full moon. Enrico moved to the courtyard avoiding the guard at the sheikh's door. He had some pieces of chicken, a canteen of water and the blanket from his bed. From the shadows he could see that the main gate was open and only two sentries were visible. Carefully he made his way to the postern gate. It was unlocked, it opened noiselessly and he slipped into the oasis. Using all available cover he made his way to the track. Only once did he falter as a camel's bray broke the silence. The sand dunes cast great shadows and Enrico used these to walk parallel with the track until, on looking back, the fortress was almost out of sight. He stepped onto the track and began to move steadily along it. He rested, nibbled at the food and drank sparingly. Just before dawn he found the track straddled by a sand dune. To save time he climbed the dune and slid down the other side... there was no track! As the sun rose Enrico looked about him. The track had disappeared, he chose to turn right in search of it. The temperature began to rise, he stopped. All he could see was sand dunes, he drank from the canteen and ploughed on. He came across a skeleton, it had been an animal of some kind, its bones were bleached, Enrico shuddered. He saw something between two dunes, full of hope he quickened his pace. He found himself looking at the remains of an old car. The bonnet, engine and wheels were missing but there was a little shade and Enrico used it. He decided to move on, this car was a sign of life, he reasoned. He drank from the canteen and was dismayed to find that it was now empty. He left the car, the blanket and canteen testimony to his passing. Inevitably the sun took its toll on the body of the young Italian. Drained, exhausted by the relentless heat, he collapsed. He forced himself upright and attempted to struggle on, the ground here was flat for some miles.

Six men on horseback sat line-abreast on top of a sand dune. They were covered against the rays of the sun, they all carried rifles and bandoliers; a packhorse and an unsaddled horse completed the group. The horses' hooves were wrapped in cloth to muffle any sound of their presence. Eyes watched as the figure tottered and fell. One of the horsemen gathered himself to ride his horse down the slope but the leader of the party raised his arm quickly, the rider settled down again. Twice more the tortured man got to his feet and twice more he crashed to the sand, then he began to crawl. Mahmoud looked at Ahmed, nodded, and, as one the horsemen spurred their mounts to the rescue. Water filtered into Enrico's throat, the precious liquid life supplied in just the right quantity by Ahmed. Willing hands lifted Enrico's body across the spare horse, ropes tied around him to keep him on board.

He dreamed of sand, of an animal that lay on its side breathing heavily, he saw a car speeding down a track. He saw the fan turning slowly, then it was gone. His eyes were full of sweat; he looked into the sun, felt its heat and suddenly returned to the land of the living.

"Welcome back, Rico," it was Mahmoud.

He found it hard to speak.

"Rest, now, you will soon recover from your escapade."

It was some hours before he sat up. Ever present, Mahmoud gave Enrico tea. He looked round, neatly folded on a chair was a blanket and, on top of it, a canteen, he looked at Mahmoud.

"To remind you of your folly."

"You knew, Mahmoud?"

"It was expected."

"Did you follow me?"

Mahmoud nodded.

"How far did I get?"

"We lost count of the circles you made but the ride was short, around seven miles."

Enrico lay back, a valuable lesson learned, his glance at Mahmoud was full of utmost respect.

Mahmoud bustled into the room with unusual haste. Enrico looked up, Mahmoud had a robe over his arm.

"Put this on, Rico, you have an audience with the sheikh."

The robe was beautifully embroidered with animal images, a camel and horse in gold thread on a dark blue background.

"Come, Rico, and remember, stay behind me as we enter the chamber, we must kneel and bow – follow my lead, understood?"

"Yes, Mahmoud."

"And stayed bowed until you are ordered to stand."

Enrico nodded.

He was nervous as the doors were opened and he moved between the guards into the room. It was large, as he expected, but there was no display of richness here. Rows of chairs down each wall, two cabinets and a desk were positioned to leave the centre of the room empty. The sheikh sat on an ornate chair on a small platform. Mahmoud glanced at Enrico and they both assumed the required posture, Enrico became impatient as a long silence ensued but a word from the sheikh saved him from any embarrassment. He was able to study the sheikh who rose and stepped down from the platform. He was taller than Enrico anticipated and, although he was clean-shaven and wore a full headdress, there was something familiar about him. He wore a caftan, a long loose garment which was elaborately patterned. His eyes moved over Enrico slowly, evaluating, they were shrewd but open, bearing no hostility. He spoke to Mahmoud in his own language, he would act as interpreter. The voice was soft but there was a trace of steel present, here was a man used to being obeyed. He was obviously aware of Enrico's desert exploit.

"You have recovered from your 'walk' in the night?"

"Yes, thank you."

The sheikh began to stroll, his hands clasped behind his back. He looked at Enrico.

"You grew vines and produced wine in Italy, I understand."

"That is true."

The sheikh stroked his chin as if in deep thought.

"You are a man who knows how to care for your vines, the food and amount of water they need. I have a large herd of horses, among them two Arabs, my own personal mounts. I need someone to care for them, will you do it?"

Enrico looked at Mahmoud then at the sheikh.

"Yes, I will."

The sheikh nodded, "You will need assistance."

Again Enrico looked to Mahmoud, "Can I have the boy who brings my food, Mahammad?"

Mahmoud conversed with his master. The sheikh gave his approval, the audience was at an end. Mahoud backed from the room, bowing, Enrico copied him. When they were alone Enrico questioned Mahmoud.

"Who is the sheikh?"

"He is a Berber, as we all are. A descendant of his was a highly successful pirate on the Barbary coast but they were driven from the sea by American and European navies. The descendant came into the desert, found this oasis and settled here."

"He looked familiar."

"He would, Ahmed is his brother, the sheikh is the thinker, the administrator, Ahmed more the military man, the leader in the field."

Enrico frowned, "Who do you have to fight?"

"You will learn more as your education progresses."

For many weeks Enrico wrestled with the Berber language but Ahmed was a man of infinite patience. Very little Berber is written, making it hard to learn but mainly thanks to the perseverance of both teacher and pupil Enrico began to improve. He used Mahammad as a sounding board to good effect. Their friendship grew as they tended the sheikh's horses, Enrico developed a true affection for the Arab pair. He exercised them, gave them small treats and talked to them. He took easily to riding horses and Ahmed taught him the ability to use a rifle on horseback. He took a little longer to master the camel, causing great laughter as he tumbled into the sand on numerous occasions, but he triumphed eventually. Enrico favoured the loincloth when outdoors and his body darkened, more and more frequently his sandals remained in his room and his feet toughened. He grew his hair long but chose to stay clean-shaven. As his demeanour changed so he became accepted by his Berber compatriots.

As Mahmoud had predicted, he was invited to play football. He found his fellow players highly skilled and there were always spectators in large numbers. He was initiated into the game of boules, a French version played on any surface. His moment came when a set of dominoes appeared, he quickly became the local top dog. Enrico derived great pleasure from traditional music called Rai. Instruments such as lutes, various types of drum and clackers, similar to castanets, were played, but very often women sang with trilling, high-pitched voices accompanied only by the clapping of hands. Dancing was popular, Enrico declined any invitation to join in this pastime.

Mahmoud introduced him to the dinar but he would seldom use the Algerian currency. Ahmed led Enrico through the black tents. Here he discovered a hive of activity. He saw weavers at work producing beautiful carpets. Craftsmen and women produced jewellery, swords and daggers; a thin desert grass, Esparto, was being used to create baskets, sandals and ropes – here was the real currency. The last tent revealed six jeeps, cans of petrol and workbench complete with tools, Enrico noted the armed guard looking out into the desert.

"Wear your best robe, Rico, the sheikh wants to see you," Mahmoud said.

Enrico did not feel so nervous this time, he made the required act of obeisance with confident ease.

"Mahmoud, Enrico, rise, sit."

The use of his name surprised Enrico but he remained expressionless.

"You have learned the basics of our language, I hear."

"Yes."

"Excellent, I have watched you with the horses especially my Arabs, they have more love for you than their master now."

There was no reproach in the voice.

"Our masters, the French, are paying us a visit soon, our outposts have marked their approach. They are French Foreign Legion troops from Sidi-bel-Abbes. It is reported that Colonel Armand Lascelles is among them, he is a great exponent of French colonisation in this country, especially with a gun!"

There was no hiding the bitterness in the sheikh's voice on this occasion.

"You may ask why he still lives, the answer is the human cost if he were to be assassinated, but enough of this, have you any questions, Enrico?"

"When can I return to Italy?"

"That is for Allah to say."

"Do you always hide behind Allah?"

At this Mahoud leapt to his feet but the sheikh raised his hand.

"Sit, Mahmoud, it is only natural that Enrico should want to return to his homeland."

Mahmoud threw a withering look at Enrico and, reluctantly, resumed his seat.

The sheikh looked earnestly at Enrico.

"Listen to your teachers, build on life's knowledge, learn to be patient, would it be that I could hide behind Allah when the French guns arrive."

Eyes surveyed the desert as small clouds of sand on the horizon heralded the arrival of the Foreign Legion. Everyone stopped work to watch the convoy sweep into the courtyard. There were three transport vehicles and two jeeps all bearing the French tricolor. Amid shouted commands troops leapt from the vehicles and formed orderly lines, standing to attention. As relative quiet returned, a man left the leading jeep. He pulled his jacket down to its correct position and adjusted his cap. Tall, slim, immaculate, he betrayed no sign of having travelled through a hot, arid desert. His thin face bore little effects from the sun, he was thin-lipped, had a small moustache, a patrician's nose and ice-blue eyes.

"Dismiss the men, sergeant-major, let them relax in the shade," his voice was not loud but held a steely, authoritarian timbre.

The man saluted, "Yes, sir."

Colonel Lascelles looked up at the windows before him. He saw the sheikh looking down at him, their eyes met. Lascelles moved smartly to the steps, he really hates me, he thought.

The sheikh and Lascelles sat opposite each other. A small delegation of Berbers stood behind the sheikh including Mahmoud and Enrico. Wine had been produced for the Colonel, Enrico noted the absence of respect on both sides.

"Why are you here, Colonel?"

"To inspect your domain, sheikh."

"You mean search, Colonel."

The Colonel stood up and walked to the window.

"You could put it like that I suppose."

"Why?"

"I have to assure the French government that this is a peaceful settlement, not a nest of vipers."

"I see," the sheikh's voice was controlled.

"There will be no damage, no harm to anyone unless resistance is met, of course."

"Of course."

"So it will commence," the Colonel turned and strode from the room.

Enrico looked at Mahmoud, he caught the glance and put a single finger to his lips, Enrico remained silent. The search was thorough but there was no damage as promised. The metal door to the building in the courtyard was opened, the interior was empty, the jeeps and fuel were well hidden. The smell of food assailed the nostrils, the legionnaires ate in a black tent, their commander dined with the sheikh. Conversation was light as both men avoided the political issues of the day. Lascelles was allocated a guest room, his men camped in the desert. It was five o'clock the following morning when a bugle woke the troops and most of the population. Lascelles ate a small breakfast washed down with coffee. The sheikh had taken coffee with Lascelles who rose from the table, he bowed.

"Thank you, sheikh, your hospitality was first class, as usual."

The sheikh returned the bow, "Safe journey, Colonel."

Lascelles smiled, turned on his heel and marched out to his men. At exactly six o'clock the lead jeep went through the fort gate. The convoy formed, on the move, and followed the track, soon disappearing from view. The sheikh was standing by the window long after the legionnaires had departed, deep in thought.

Months and years went by. Enrico learned Algerian history from both Mahmoud and Ahmed, their main topic being the colonisation of the country by the French and the number of foreigners occupying sizeable areas of their land. Both men made no effort to hide their bitter resentment. To his surprise and pleasure his audiences with the sheikh became more frequent. He gave Enrico permission to enter one of his horses in the many races held on a course around the football pitch. It was no contest, the Arabs thrashed the opposition and Enrico welcomed the plaudits. Gamely he took part in camel races but invariably, at some stage, he fell off, causing great amusement among the spectators. Enrico learned about the environment. Ahmed taught him how to find water and warned him of the dangers in the desert such as snakes and insects that inhabited old buildings, caves or rocks. Mahmoud presented him with a stout pair of boots for his protection. He was introduced to the Tuareg, the indigenous people of the Sahara. Sometimes they were referred to as the 'blue men' because of their indigo-coloured headdress. They came in caravans laden with goods. Enrico watched them trading with interest.

"Get to know the Tuareg, Rico, they are our life-blood with their caravans criss-crossing the desert."

Enrico nodded.

Armand Lascelles came on one of his frequent visits, as always his searches revealed nothing. It was shortly after one of these intrusions that Enrico saw changes taking place. Arabs he had never seen before visited the fort. The guards on the sheikh's quarters and the ramparts were doubled, sentries were positioned at the postern gate. The main gate remained closed, opened only when necessary. The Tuareg caravans brought guns and ammunition. Then several lorries entered the fortress and it was stripped of every valuable item, furniture, ornaments and carpets. Late that same day Enrico was summoned to the sheikh's quarters. He joined Mahmoud, Ahmed, Mahammad and a group of men selected from the camp. They sat in a half circle in front of the sheikh who was standing on his platform, all eyes focussed on him.

"Welcome to you all on a fateful day. There is going to be a war," he paused as a murmur passed through the assembly. "An organisation, the Front de Liberation Nationale, has been formed to co-ordinate military operations against the French oppressor. The terrain here is unsuitable for guerrilla warfare, we will be moving into our traditional territory, the Atlas Mountains. Mahmoud, you are to go to Algiers as part of a FLN committee, you leave tomorrow with Mahammad who will be taking men, jeeps and fuel to various destinations. Ahmed will be responsible for breaking camp, we must depart as soon as possible, leaving no one behind. Enrico this is not your fight…"

"I will stand with you," Enrico said.

The sheikh nodded, "Then you take care of the horses."

The meeting was at an end, it was August 1954.

Colonel Lascelles stood on the sand dune surveying the fortress through binoculars, he passed them to one of his officers.

"What do you make of it?"

"It appears to be deserted, not a stick left."

Lascelles frowned and looked around, the desert was hot, empty.

"Send in a dozen men, tell them to watch for booby traps and check the oasis water."

An hour later Lascelles made his own inspection, the place was bare. From the ramparts he could see a wide swathe of hoof and footmarks disappearing into the desert. He turned to one of his lieutenants, an arm sweeping out to indicate the fortress.

"Burn it," he said.

Some fifty miles north-east of the fort were the ruins of a village. Here El-Quasimi divided his people into two groups. Men, women, children and the elderly erected the black tents and would resume normal life unmolested, he prayed. Two hundred fighting men on horseback and a number of pack animals, El-Quasimi at their head, moved on. Some days later Enrico noticed the changing landscape. The desert gave way to more and more vegetation, he saw crops growing. Ahead he caught sight of mountain tops. One more day and he could see the whole range. He would soon discover the existence of fertile valleys, agriculture, livestock, dense forests and many mountain passes. The force moved into a forest area and pitched camp. Sentries kept watch and El-Quasimi allowed fires so that his troops could enjoy hot food and drink, this would become a rare event in the coming years. Two days later ten men rode into the camp, their presence on the mountain had come under observation long before their arrival. Enrico looked at Ahmed.

"Mahmoud's men, they will have radios and ammunition."

"They were expected?"

"Yes, my brother will be happy, now he has communications we can start work."

The sheikh divided his guerrillas into four groups, three headed by his chosen commanders, Ahmed, Enrico and Mahammad; the remaining men maintained supplies of food and horses from the land. Wisely he allowed his men to become accustomed to the terrain. Radio messages came in at regular intervals and El-Quasimi began to deploy his groups to locate and assess the strength and weaknesses of the enemy. A map took shape showing the positions of French military installations and, on November 1st 1954, the men from the mountains joined a series of attacks that took place right across the country.

Enrico took his troops out after dark. Quickly and quietly they surrounded an installation built to protect a supply road through the mountains. Men slipped from their horses and used the cover of darkness to get close to and successfully eliminate the sentries. Seconds later a fuel tank exploded and the small garrison came from their slumber and out into the open, Enrico released his mounted force. Blood-curling yells split the air as the Berbers rode at their adversaries and shots rang out. Enrico spurred his horse forward and almost at once saw a French soldier aiming his rifle. His reaction was swift, he killed his first man. None of the garrison survived and personal items were stripped from the bodies. Enrico gathered the men and made for home, five of their number would never fight again!

El-Quasimi made full use of the environment. Food, water and horses were available to him. He used the forest as cover against the threat from the air. Radio messages from the FLN committee provided a basis for his attacks. Military bases faced night assaults, ambushes in mountain passes deterred French probes for some time. Casualties were inevitable but there were always recruits to be found. There was little time to relax, the Berbers were constantly on the move to maintain the upper hand in the mountain range.

Elsewhere the war took on an ominous trend. Civilians began to suffer as bombs exploded in public places. The French military retaliated and many Algerians paid the ultimate price. News came through that Mahmoud was dead. An FLN committee meeting had been trapped in a building by French troops, they systematically destroyed the structure and the occupants. The French brought thousands of soldiers into Algeria, attacks against all guerrilla units escalated.

The convoy moved steadily through the long mountain pass. The military had reopened the supply routes, they intended to grind the mountain guerrillas out of action. It rained heavily, there would be no air cover today. Anxious eyes roved the landscape, their edginess was well founded. A radio message found Mahammad and thirty men well placed to take on the convoy. They were deployed quickly and the French drove into the ambush. Practised riflemen blasted the windscreen and tyres of the lead vehicle. The battle was short, the guerrilla fire was accurate, the French were caught in a deadly crossfire. Mahammad's force began to strip the convoy of its contents which would be of some use to them.

They found the girl in an ambulance at the rear of the convoy, she was brought to Mahammad. His eyes moved over the slim girl with long fair hair and blue eyes and frowned, she looked vaguely familiar.

"Bring her along."

She could speak English so Enrico was called to interpret. She had arrived blindfold and covered from the rain and was standing in El-Quasimi's tent.

"You have a name?"

"Michelle Lascelles – Doctor."

The assembled commanders looked at each other.

"Are you the daughter of Colonel Armand Lascelles?"

"That is so, he will come looking for me."

"Of that there is little doubt but meanwhile you can be of service to us, we have medical supplies."

"Why should I look after your casualties?"

"Because you're a doctor," Enrico said.

"You're not an Arab are you?"

The question caught Enrico off guard, Michelle Lascelles was tending a wounded man.

"No, I'm Italian."

"Why are you here?"

"I was kidnapped and brought here some years ago."

"Why?"

He shrugged, "I do not know."

"Have you tried to escape?"

"Yes, in the desert, it was a total disaster."

"It is my duty to escape, Enrico."

"Then you will be of no use to anyone."

"Why?"

"You will be dead!"

He fought, she tried to save lives. They talked, learned about each other's lives and their native countries. She taught him French and she began to grasp some of the Berber language. They became close friends but not lovers, there was no space or time in this war.

Reports came in that military activity in the mountain passes was on the increase. Noticeably more aircraft came over the forest. The sheikh was given food for thought when he realised that his directives were coming from Morocco and Tunisia! Wisely he cut the number of operations, amassed quantities of food and water and conserved ammunition. His men set booby traps at the lower edge of the forest primarily to sound a warning of enemy advance. Two days later the dawn came bright and clear, so did the French! Steadily the infantry came on and aircraft began to circle, the guerrillas began an orderly retreat. They went higher and higher, behind them the French aircraft dropped bombs, fired rockets and napalm, hoping to envelope the unseen enemy. The Berbers kept their discipline and their knowledge of the mountains proved vital. El-Quasimi led his troops with consummate skill. He rested the men as often as he could, they ate and drank sparingly, at times they walked, easing the horses' workload. By nightfall the force was still intact, silence pervaded the countryside, pursuit had ceased. The following day the French forces continued the hunt. Eventually the ground forces neared the summit of their designated mountain. Fingers tightened on weapons, eyes constantly searched, the advance slowed. Aircraft passed overhead but no sightings were forthcoming. The French commander in the field halted the advance. Minutes later a scouting party spread out and stealthily approached the mountain top. Each of them awaited sudden death, it never came. Sometime during the night any enemy that had been here was gone. Yesterday they had seen signs of very recent habitation, today the mountain was empty!

The French had complete control in Algeria. El-Quasimi buried his weapons and ammunition. His men spread out over the mountains, agricultural work was plentiful. Michelle Lascelles was delivered back to her countrymen, the gracious sheikh thanked her for her services, Enrico was absent when she left. His commanders about him, El Quasimi moved deep into the mountains and safety. They built huts and produced crops. They had retained their radios and daily listened for news. The Algerian War of Independence gained an international profile. French colonists and some military twice rebelled against their own administration, the conflict and its cost became unpopular in France itself. Finally a political solution was found and a ceasefire ensued. A referendum held in 1962 overwhelmingly voted for independence, many French then left the country.

Seven bedraggled horsemen sat on their mounts and looked at the remains of the fort. The wooden parts of the structure were charred or ashes. The walls were blackened and had cracked in places from the heat. Little vegetation had managed to grow but there were signs of habitation. Further inspection revealed that the mosque had not been put to the torch but had been stripped of its furniture. The oasis was filled with sand, this would soon be dug out again. Sheikh El-Quasimi turned and looked at his six comrades, all that remained of the original two hundred fighters.

"Lascelles," he said bitterly.

The hum came from the north-east and grew in intensity. The horsemen wheeled their mounts and sought the cause of the commotion, their quest was soon answered. Heads appeared above the dunes, then bodies, horses and camels. Women and children trotted alongside, some leading beasts laden with equipment. Some men on horseback broke away and headed for the fort.

"The Berbers are back," shouted Ahmed.

At the sight of their sheikh, the column of humanity speeded up. The two groups met and shouting, greetings and back-slapping seemed to go on endlessly. Gradually some order was restored and the black tents began to appear. Enrico looked at the fort.

"What happens now, Ahmed?"

Ahmed followed his gaze.

"Everything will be as it was, we will find more stone and the Tuareg will provide the wood."

El-Quasimi turned to face Enrico.

"You have been like a son to me, Rico, over these many years but now is the time for you to return to your own people."

Enrico was speechless.

"Find his old clothes, Ahmed, they may fit him."

Ahmed smiled, "The problem will be but a minute one," he clapped Enrico heartily across the shoulder. For some hours Enrico pondered on his life in the desert. He had been here for seventeen years but Italy beckoned and he would answer her call.

Sheikh El-Quasimi looked at Enrico. His hair had been cut and he wore the dress of his country but his skin was almost black. The sheikh stepped forward and clasped Enrico to him, then they shook hands. He turned and scooped two items from the table. He gave Enrico a camel-skin sheath from which he took a sabre. It bore intricate, hand-engraved decorations.

"This is beautiful, master."

"You may remember a car in the desert where you once sought shade."

Enrico remembered, he looked up.

"The engine provided the necessary metal."

The second item was a bag.

"Take good are of this, it contains your future. Goodbye, Enrico."

No further words were spoken, Enrico bowed deeply and left the tent. Mahammad was waiting in a jeep, he climbed aboard. He soon became aware that the whole camp had come to say farewell. The crowd cheered and waved him on his way and as the jeep broke clear a solitary figure stood, his right hand raised in salute.

"Goodbye, Rico."

"Goodbye, Ahmed."

Enrico sat back in his seat and fell silent, deep in thought. Thanks to Ahmed he knew who had been responsible for his kidnap!

* * * * *

Claudia, Andrea, Guilio and the children were indoors. The afternoon was sultry, quiet, disturbed only by the twittering of birds. A man, shirt-sleeved, his jacket flung over his shoulder approached the Villa Belucchi. At his knock Claudia opened the door coming face to face with a very dark-skinned stranger. Their eyes met.

"Hello, Claudia."

She stared at him, it was the eyes that told her who he was.

"Enrico?"

"Yes, it's Enrico."

Claudia cried out and leapt at her brother, her arms encircling his neck, almost knocking him over. Andrea came to the door.

"Who is it, Claudia?"

"It's my brother... back from the dead!"

Guilio had arrived to find out what was going on.

"Father, it's Enrico!"

Guilio hesitated as if to recall a memory then he peered into Enrico's face.

"My God, it is you!"

He reached for his son, and wept. The children came and everyone started talking at once. The family gathered for food, wine and memories of the past years, the talk continued deep into the night. The following day Claudia and Enrico strolled in the gardens.

"There are things you should know."

"Such as?"

"Frederico Rinaldi owns the vineyard, Father doesn't know."

Enrico stared at his sister.

"How long?"

"Nearly seventeen years, he got us out of trouble."

"Tell me the details."

Over the next days Enrico was overwhelmed by the welcome extended by friends and employees alike. He had two cost-free evenings at the village bar. Guiseppe and Carla had aged but she still displayed her assets and almost crushed every ounce of air from his body when they met. As the furore of his homecoming died down Enrico hired a car and with the sheikh's bag beside him, set out on the road to Florence.

Frederico Rinaldi put a piece of jewellery in its cabinet and closed the door it, was nearly time to shut up shop, he turned.

"Hello, Frederico."

"Yes, can I help you?"

"I hope so, I want the Belucchi vineyard returned to its previous owner."

Frederico was taken aback, he searched the face again, his own became ashen as realisation came.

"Enrico!"

"Correct, my Algerian captors looked after me well."

Frederico's voice was strained, "You escaped?"

"No I left of my own free will, I was owed a debt."

"What if I deny any involvement in this... this conspiracy?"

"I will take you to court but I think Marcello would be most displeased."

Frederico had regained some composure.

"You, take me to court, a peasant from the fields?"

"A man of wealth returning from abroad, I made a bank manager a very happy man today."

Doubt creased Rinaldi's features.

"What exactly do you want?"

"A new contract giving Claudia ownership of the vineyard."

"It can be arranged."

"It will be arranged, Frederico, today... now!

Claudia automatically wiped her hands on her pinafore as she answered the door. A young slim girl stood on the porch.

"Yes?"

"Is this the Belucchi Villa?"

"It is."

"I'm Michelle Lascelles, I'm looking for Enrico."

"Come in, I will fetch him."

He came in, "Michelle, what... how are you?"

"I am well," her eyes twinkled, "You look great!"

Enrico became aware of his rough attire and adopted a sheepish look. Michelle chuckled then held her arms out to him. Enrico moved into the embrace... and his future.

Epilogue

ENGLAND 1945 – 1950

Joe watched as Margaret carefully wrapped the children in warm clothing, protection against the cold evening that awaited them. It was November the Fifth, bonfire night. Many people would be making their way to the mortuary. So called by local people, the mortuary was a square piece of land situated just over the canal bridge above St Paul's. There was a small, old cemetery in one corner, a set of swings, a roundabout and a see-saw. The rest of the site was empty, a welcome space for children to play on and dog-owners to let their pets run free. For some weeks now the population had been piling flammable materials in the centre of the mortuary and it rose, untouched, into the sky; soon an effigy of Guy Fawkes would be perched on top awaiting the inevitable end.

The fire had been lit when the Thompsons arrived. It was already providing warmth for the onlookers and the Thompson parents watched their children's reactions as fireworks went off. They were enthralled by the mixture of noise and colours and pointed with glee as rockets whistled up into the clear night sky. Joe gave Brian and Patricia sparklers to hold, making sure that they were well away from their faces. All too soon the blaze reached its zenith but a cheer rang out as Guy Fawkes fell into the heart of the blaze amid a cascade of sparks. The Thompson grandparents had gathered a little way behind the family. Margaret had spotted them but Maureen had put a finger to her lips, they wished to focus their attention on the children's pleasure. Afterwards came a swift family reunion and Harold invited everyone back to the house for a night-cap, this would consist of warm milk for the children and cocoa for the adults.

Joe had been let out of prison six months early. He had kept out of trouble and reaped the reward. Harold saw no such parallel for David. He had intimidated both prison staff and inmates and had been attacked twice, the second time he and the wheelchair had been tipped over. Immediately after the trial Harold had spoken to Vera Lewis and together they had persuaded George to take over the shop again. At first he had baulked at the idea, pleading old age but really afraid of local reaction. Eventually he agreed to give it a try with the condition that Joe would replace him on his return, Harold smiled, that had been the second part of the plan. George need not have worried, his old customers welcomed the atmosphere, a place where neighbours met and passed the time of day and freely conversed with George himself.

Gradually the personal and material debris of war were cleared away. In the corridors of power reforms took place. Notably many institutions and industries came under public ownership including the Bank of England. Later the National Health Service was launched. The public in general supported the Labour government. Employment was high, wages good and leisure outlets were substantial. Dance halls were popular, energetic young people did the jitterbug, introduced by the American armed forces, alongside the regular English styles. Cinema was readily available. Celia Johnson, Deborah Kerr, Betty Grable, Lionel Barrymore, Bing Crosby, Rex Harrision, Alec Guinness, Laurence Olivier and Charlie Chaplin, among many others, became household names. Entertainer Nat King Cole was at this time a jazz pianist, and a young man by the name of Frank Sinatra was charming the girls known as 'bobbysoxers' – the wearing of ankle socks was in vogue. On the sporting front racing driver Juan Manuel Fangio and his Maserati hit the headlines. Trouble-free football matches took place at Villa

Park, Highbury and Old Trafford stadiums hosting a total of sixty thousand spectators every week. Close to home enterprising public houses had darts, dominoes, quoits, table skittles and playing card teams. Many featured in local leagues. Many pubs had a skittle alley – a source of noise, enthusiasm and the consumption of alcoholic beverages. Quiet board games included draughts and chess. In the home itself radio was already well established but it was now that long-playing records came onto the scene. Holidays were much improved for the men as bikini swimming costumes appeared on the beaches as a pleasurable diversion.

So life in England settled down once more, the working-man always wondering what new changes he would see. The war had inevitably changed many lives in diverse ways. Those who had fought in battle locked away the memories, someone would broadcast or write about them anyway but for now everything looked reasonably rosy, only time would tell.